Siena
Summer

Siena
Summer

by Ann Chandler

VANCOUVER   LONDON

Distribution and representation in Canada by
Publishers Group Canada • www.pgcbooks.ca

Distribution and representation in the UK by
Turnaround • www.turnaround-uk.com

Released in USA Spring 2009

Printed in Canada on 100% ancient forest friendly paper.
2 4 6 8 10 9 7 5 3 1

Cataloguing-in-Publication Data for this book
is available from The British Library.

Library and Archives Canada Cataloguing in Publication

Chandler, Ann, 1952-
    Siena summer / Ann Chandler.

ISBN 978-1-896580-17-3

    I. Title.

PS8605.H356S54 2008   jC813'.6   C2008-902865-1

*This book is dedicated to
Shyla, Cheyenne, Dustin and Callum.
—A.C.*

*The publisher wishes to thank
Luigi Benni, Luca Salice and Nadia Zonis
for their help with the Italian phrases.*

The publisher acknowledges the support of the Canada Council for the Arts.

 **Canada Council Conseil des Arts
for the Arts du Canada**

*The publisher also wishes to thank the Government of British Columbia for the
financial support it has extended through the book publishing tax credit program
and the British Columbia Arts Council.*

 BRITISH COLUMBIA
ARTS COUNCIL
Supported by the Province of British Columbia

*The publisher also acknowledges the financial support of the Government of
Canada through the Book Publishing Industry Development Program (BPIDP)
and the Association for the Export of Canadian Books (AECB) for our publishing
activities.*

Canadä

Chapter One

The Siena countryside was breathtaking. The narrow road twisted and turned. Neatly trained grapevines faded from view, then reappeared on the next hill. Row upon row of olive trees were broken here and there by stone cottages. Angela's Uncle Giorgio gave her a running commentary on each farm they passed, outlining the marriages, divorces, births and deaths of each family.

"This," he said with a sweep of his arm, "is Tuscany, Angie."

Angela watched a dapple-grey horse gallop through a distant field. His long tail streamed behind him as he ran. He kicked up his heels and tossed his head. Angela couldn't take her eyes off him as they drove by. "What a beautiful horse!" she exclaimed, turning to her uncle.

"Everybody knows that horse." He shook his head. "That's Tempesta, a crazy horse!"

"Who does he belong to?"

"That's the Barazza *allevamento*—a horse ranch. Maybe you don't remember. You visit here with your mother when you were small. Many of Barazza's horses have raced in the *Palio*. It's the biggest event in Siena. This is the best time to visit. This year with a little divine luck our neighbourhood *contrada*, the Unicorns, will win. For four years in a row, we have drawn a slow horse." He grasped the small icon of the Virgin Mary swinging from the rear-view mirror and brought it to his lips. "Divine Mary, Mother of God, bless the Unicorns with a fast horse."

"Could we stop and see the horses?" Angela asked, excited at the prospect. Although she had only arrived in Italy the week before, she had already begun to miss the stables and the horses back home in Canada.

"Sure," Giorgio said, smiling at her. "Barazza is a good friend of mine."

Giorgio turned the truck into a narrow lane, sped up a shaded driveway that led to an old farmhouse and came to a halt in a cloud of dust. The old house was flanked on one side by a grove of olive trees and on the other by a fenced paddock where several horses grazed. Behind the house, a little to the right, were the stables. As her uncle turned off the engine, a tall man appeared in the doorway, squinting into the late-afternoon sun. His thick dark hair glinted in the light, and he walked with purpose.

"Ah, Giorgio!" he called out in a strong voice.

Giorgio opened the truck door, stepped out and extended his hand. "Cesare, it's good to see you," he said.

"And you," Barazza said, grasping Giorgio's hand. "Is this Angela, Kate's daughter?" he asked, peering into the window.

Giorgio nodded proudly. "This is our Angela."

"You're all grown up," Barazza said in English. "Your aunt and uncle are so happy you have come to visit."

Angela smiled and climbed out of the truck.

"You look very much like your mother," Barazza continued. "How is she?"

"She's fine," Angela replied.

"Angela wanted to stop and see the horses," Giorgio said.

"Certainly, certainly. Make yourself at home."

"You go ahead and look at the horses, Angela, while Cesare and I discuss the Palio," Giorgio said as he followed Barazza to the house.

Angela wandered over to the paddock and leaned on the fence, feeling the intensity of the sun on her back. She ran her fingers through her hair, trying to smooth the inevitable stray wisps that always seemed to stick up in all the wrong places. She was thankful she had cut her hair short before leaving Vancouver, even though her mother had been upset when she had seen it. It was much easier to take care of in the heat.

Angela's last words to her mother had been harsh, and she was secretly glad to be away for a while. Their relationship had alternated between stony silences and yelling matches since the death of Angela's father. Her mother had reacted to becoming a widow by withdrawing from the world. Angela wondered if she'd ever again have the mother she had once known. She missed her old life when the three of them had been together.

Angela spied Tempesta, the grey dapple that she'd seen from the road. He was galloping with several other horses along the fence on the far side of the paddock. The allevamento was definitely a horse's paradise, with plush green fields that stretched for miles. Tempesta easily outdistanced the others. He had a proud way of holding his head up that made Angela think of the Lipizzaner stallions from Vienna.

The dapple was followed by a tall raw-boned mare the colour of chocolate. Her heavy hooves thudded across the turf, and her long thick neck stretched out. She could almost keep up with Tempesta as he raced around the paddock, but it was obvious that it took great effort. When Tempesta neared Angela, he stopped in his tracks, blowing sharp gusts of air out his nostrils. As the clumsy mare thundered past, the dapple fixed his eyes on Angela. His gaze never faltered as she bent down and slid through the fence. His coat quivered and his head bobbed up and down.

When Angela extended her hand, Tempesta tossed his head and snorted, eyeing her warily. His nostrils twitched, but he didn't bolt. Closer and closer Angela edged, all the while murmuring softly, "Don't be afraid. I won't hurt you."

She reached out to touch his velvety nose. Suddenly, Tempesta snorted and galloped away.

Annoyed, Angela turned and saw a tall young man approaching the paddock. He had broad shoulders and thick dark hair that curled at his collar.

"Wow! That's impressive! He rarely lets strangers approach him. You must have a special touch."

"How did you know I speak English?" Angela asked, climbing back over the paddock fence. Since she'd arrived in Siena, she'd struggled with Italian, trying to remember what little her mother had taught her.

"I heard you talking with Barazza," he said, smiling and offering her his hand. "I'm Tony."

"Angela," she replied, placing her hand in his. "Do you work here?" His grip was warm and firm.

"I come to ride, to practise for the Palio," he said, holding her hand tightly. "I'm a *fantino*, a jockey. I ride the racing circuit all around Tuscany, and this year I'm going to win the Palio." He let go of her hand and nodded toward the dapple prancing across the field. "He's a real devil," he said with a deep throaty laugh.

"There's something special about him," Angela said, gazing at Tempesta.

"He's fast, but too unpredictable, too temperamental." Tony leaned forward and rested his arms on the fence next to Angela's as Tempesta cantered past them, tossing his head from side to side. "He'd make a good racehorse—too bad."

Tony turned to Angela. "Do you ride back home?"

"Yes, I...I do," she stammered, annoyed at herself for feeling intimidated by this lean young man with the brazen attitude.

"Your father own a ranch?"

"No, we live in the city." She lowered her eyes to the ground, scuffing the toe of her shoe in the soil. She could picture her father's face, every detail as sharp as the last time she saw him. "My dad died last year. He was a high-school teacher."

"Oh." Tony touched her arm. "I'm sorry to hear that."

"I'm a show jumper," Angela said, changing the subject. "There's a stable near my house. I've been riding there for years. I'm saving up to buy my own horse."

"Have you won any trophies?"

"A few." She smiled at the thought of her wall back home filled with row upon row of first and second place ribbons.

Suddenly, a movement near the house caught her attention as sunlight glinted off something metal. A figure, partially concealed by the late afternoon shadows, slid out of the back door of the house onto the brick patio. It was a young woman in a wheelchair. Her dark hair fell in a thick braid over her right shoulder, and she wore a pink floral skirt. Angela couldn't help staring at her.

Just then, Giorgio and Barazza emerged from the house. Angela watched them walk over to the truck, but when she glanced back, the girl in the wheelchair was gone.

She looked over at Tony. He seemed so confident, so much more self-assured than the boys she knew back home.

"I'd better go," she said, and turned to leave.

"Wait!" Tony said, placing his hand on her arm. "How long are you staying?"

"I'm here for a few more weeks. Then I go back for my last school year," she answered, aware that his hand still lingered on her arm. "Maybe I'll see you around."

"Angela! Come!" Giorgio waved at her. She smiled at Tony, then turned and walked toward the truck, her skin tingling from his touch.

"Well, what do you think of my horses?" Barazza asked as Angela walked up to the two men standing by the truck.

"They're beautiful," Angela answered.

"I see you've met Siena's famous jockey," Barazza said with a chuckle.

"Tony? Yes, we met."

"Your uncle tells me you're very good with horses," Barazza said.

Angela nodded. "I'm a show jumper."

"I could use some help around here, if you're interested," Barazza said.

"With the horses?" Angela brightened.

"I need someone to exercise them." He tilted his head toward the house. "My daughter Catarina used to do that, before she had the accident. She can't ride just yet. I'd be happy to pay you."

Angela looked at her uncle, who smiled and nodded his approval. "Sure!" she said. "When can I start?"

"How about tomorrow?"

Chapter Two

The next morning, Angela sat with a cup of coffee at one of the crowded sidewalk tables outside the small bakery her aunt and uncle owned. She felt relieved to escape the heat of the kitchen. *Even the air in Italy is different,* she thought. She was amazed at how a simple horse race could occupy the interest of a whole city, not just at the time of the race, but, according to Giorgio, for the whole year! Many of the shops and homes hung Palio pictures on their walls. There were Palio souvenirs on sale for the tourists, everything from scarves to pencils. All the shops were decorated with the colours of their neighbourhood contrada.

The bakery was alive with Palio chatter. She watched a group of round-faced men speaking animatedly, slamming their fists on the tables until their tiny espresso cups bounced.

She glanced at her watch. *Tony should be here any minute to pick me up and take me to Barazza's.*

Watching the customers munching pastries and sipping tiny mugs of dark espresso coffee, Angela smiled to herself. *Italians are so passionate about everything, even something as simple as a conversation over coffee.* Their animated faces and broad gesturing amused Angela.

Angela spotted her Uncle Giorgio coming out of the bakery. He nodded to his customers and greeted them by name, wearing his usual broad grin. When he reached Angela's table, he wiped his hands on his apron and said, "Tony just called. He's going to be late. He'll be here to pick you up in half an hour."

"Thanks, Uncle," Angela said, picking up her cup and following him back inside the bakery.

Aunt Maria was busy in the kitchen, punching her hands firmly into a large mass of soft dough. She grunted and glared at her husband. "Giorgio! *Le stai permettendo di andare con quel ragazzo? No!*"

"It's all right, Mama." Giorgio waved his hand. "It will be fine."

"What did Auntie say, Uncle Giorgio?"

"Nothing, nothing, dear."

"Hmmph!" Aunt Maria grunted, still glaring at her husband. She wagged a doughy finger at him. *"Te ne pentirai!"*

Angela glanced from one face to the other, frowning. Aunt Maria obviously disapproved of something. Angela wished she could understand Italian better. She placed her cup in the sink and followed her uncle out to the front counter.

"What's Auntie talking about?" Angela asked her uncle as he placed a dozen rolls into a bag for a stout lady clutching a fistful of money.

"She's worried about you being around Tony."

"But why?"

"Aach! It's nothing. He has a reputation as a ladies' man." Giorgio shrugged.

The customer tapped her hand impatiently on the counter. "Coming, coming," Giorgio muttered.

Angela saw Tony's convertible sports car pull up in front of the bakery. He slid out from behind the wheel, looking attractive in blue jeans and a white T-shirt. She hurried to greet him, but Aunt Maria blocked the doorway with her wide body as Tony walked up.

"Buon giorno, Maria," Tony said with a smile, glancing past her at Angela.

"*Buon giorno*, Tony," Aunt Maria said firmly. "You will take good care of her, no?"

"*Sì*, Maria."

"*Sì, Maria*," Aunt Maria repeated mockingly, tipping her head from side to side. "Sì, you certainly will!" She leaned forward and fixed Tony with a solid stare. "Angela is our guest. Remember that." She turned to her husband and raised her eyebrows. "Isn't that right, Giorgio?"

"Quite right, Mama. Quite right."

"Don't worry about me, Auntie. I'll be fine," Angela said, anxious to be on her way.

Aunt Maria stepped aside.

As they dodged crazy drivers and the odd mule on the winding road from Siena to the allevamento, Tony chatted about the weather, his year living in Boston and the excitement of touring the race circuit in Tuscany.

He pulled the car up to the house and shut off the engine just as Barazza emerged to greet them. Barazza opened the car door for Angela and waved Tony away.

"Come Angela, I will show you our horses, and then you will meet Catarina."

Tony shrugged and smiled as Barazza took Angela's elbow and steered her toward the stables. When they passed the house, Angela glanced up and saw Catarina watching from a window.

The pungent smell of horses and hay greeted Angela as she and Barazza entered the cool stone and timber building. The building was old, its dirt floor well hardened from years of foot traffic, and its wall timbers thick and scarred. Inside the first stall was the chocolate mare Angela had seen on her first visit to the allevamento. She reached out and touched the mare's soft brown nose.

"That's Bella," Barazza said as he approached her stall. "She would like to be a racehorse, but she's too clumsy!" He laughed. "Eh, Bella?"

Angela stroked the mare's long neck, and then scratched the bony part behind her ears. Bella nickered, stretching out her nose and nuzzling against Angela's shirt.

The grey dapple stood sideways in the next stall. He reared and spun away as Barazza approached, pressing up against the far wall. The whites of Tempesta's eyes flashed in the gloom.

"That horse is no good. He is crazy! Nobody can do anything with him. *Pazzo!*" His fingers tapped the side of his head. "He is crazy! Come, I show you the rest of the horses."

But Angela couldn't take her eyes off Tempesta. He peered at her through a cascade of grey-white mane, bobbing his head up and down and snorting. *He doesn't look mean,* she thought, *just scared.*

Angela glanced at Barazza, who had moved on to the next stall. She looked back at Tempesta. "Don't worry," she whispered. "I'll be back."

"Forget about Tempesta," Barazza called. "Come, meet Francesco!" He gestured toward an impressive bay poking his head out from a stall on the other side of the barn. "He's a beauty!"

When Angela and Barazza had finished their tour of the stables, they went into the spacious kitchen. Tony offered them lemonade from a tall green glass pitcher. He smiled at Angela. "What did you think of the horses?" he asked.

"They're lovely," Angela answered, thinking about the dapple.

"They are," Tony said. "There have been a few Palio winners from here."

Catarina sat beside the kitchen table in her wheelchair and reached for a glass of lemonade. Angela stifled a gasp. Catarina's right calf was missing a piece of flesh, and only scarred skin stretched taught over her shin bone. Her puffy bare foot was twisted inward at an awkward angle, and the skin above her knee had been removed for grafting, leaving a thick white surface. Her left knee sported a thin angry red scar.

"Angela, this is Catarina," Barazza said, smiling at the girl in the wheelchair.

Catarina nodded curtly at Angela. "Hi," she said. Then she turned to Barazza. *"Sono stanca, papà. Vado in camera mia."* She placed the glass of lemonade in the cup holder on her wheelchair and spun around, turning her back on Angela.

"Perché non rimani a parlare con noi?" Barazza called after her, but Catarina made no reply as she disappeared through an adjoining door.

"She hasn't been the same since the accident," Barazza whispered, apologetically. "Where are the biscuits?" he muttered, rummaging through the cupboards. "Since Rosa's been gone, I can't find anything in this kitchen."

"Here," Tony said. "They're on the table."

"I've got to call Leonardo about Tempesta." Barazza stopped and looked at Tony. "Remind me to call him, will you? He's got to pick that horse up. The sooner, the better."

Angela felt a sudden jolt of panic. She looked at Barazza and her breath quickened. "Where's he going?" she asked.

"Leonardo runs the slaughterhouse," Tony said.

"Nothing can be done with him," said Barazza. "He rides with no problem, then bang! He goes crazy." He shook his head.

"But..." Angela said, "you're having him destroyed? There must be something we can do."

Barazza turned to look at Angela and placed his hands on the table. "Something terrible happened to that horse when he was younger; something that sets him off for no reason. He doesn't trust anyone. There's nothing we can do. Sometimes animals are just a danger to those around them." He shrugged and picked up the box of biscuits. "They have to go."

Angela swallowed hard.

"How many horses are you entering in the line-up for the Palio time trials this year?" Tony spoke up.

"Only Francesco. The rest are not ready." Barazza thrust a plate full of biscuits at Angela. "Have a biscuit," he said gruffly. "Your job will be to exercise Francesco. Oh, and give Bella a workout too. Leave the rest to run in the pasture. We'll start training them in the fall for next year's race."

He sat down and looked at Angela. His voice softened. "It is good that you have come. Catarina needs a friend." He ran his hand through his thick hair. "She is very lonely since her mother died. She'll come around. Give her time."

Angela nodded. "I might as well get started with the horses."

She left the house, entered the cool stable and waited for her eyes to adjust to the gloom. She took a deep breath, savouring the familiar scent of horses and straw, and then looked up. The ancient stone walls, supported by massive timbers, rose two storeys in height. Angela spied the tack room down at the end of the hall, past an empty stall with a wooden sign above it bearing the name *Figaro* carved in elaborate script. A row of pigeons lined the long crossbeam above her head, ducking and cooing as Angela passed underneath. She entered the tack room, took a curry-comb from the row hanging across the back wall and closed the door behind her as she left.

Tempesta pricked his ears forward and whinnied gently when he heard Angela's footsteps. Curious, she approached his stall from the side and reached out her hand, but he tossed his head and backed away, flattening his ears. His skin quivered.

"Easy boy," she murmured. "I won't hurt you." The gangly mare in the next stall snorted and stared at her. "Don't worry, girl. I'll get to you in a minute."

She wanted to try brushing Tempesta first. "Tempesta," she whispered to herself. Her Italian was not great, but she knew what the word meant in English. "Storm," she said out loud. "I'm going to call you *Storm*."

As Angela carefully opened the stall door, Storm backed away from her, snorting. He bounced his head up and down. Angela closed the door behind her and pressed her back against it. She stood still, allowing him to get used to her presence.

"You look like a beautiful storm cloud," she said softly. He twitched one ear forward, as if he were listening to her. Then he snorted a warning to her not to come any closer.

Just then Angela heard a voice.

"You'd better be careful; he's unpredictable."

Turning, she saw the slim girl in the wheelchair coming down the aisle between the stalls. Her chair made a crunching sound on the straw-covered floor.

"He spooks," Catarina continued, stopping the chair outside the stall. "When we bought him at the auction, the owner said we were saving him from being turned into horsemeat." She gazed wistfully at Storm. "There was something about him, something special. So I talked Papa into buying him."

She pushed her chair closer, secured the brakes, reached up, grasped the post and pulled herself out of the chair. She wobbled and swayed in an effort to maintain her balance. Angela thought she might fall and instinctively reached over to grab her arm.

"I'm fine," Catarina said, waving her away. She leaned on the stall door. The dapple nickered gently and bobbed his head. "Hello, Tempesta," she murmured softly, reaching out her hand. He stepped gingerly forward, stretched out his neck and rubbed his nose against her outstretched palm. "You're a good boy, aren't you?" She smiled. "You didn't mean to hurt me, did you?" She glanced at Angela, then back at the horse. "He's fast. I thought he could run in the Palio. I thought it would just take somebody who was willing to work with him. You know, be gentle and kind and patient. I still think that. But after he threw me and trampled on my leg, Papa wanted to destroy him."

"*Quel cavallo è pazzo!*" Tony said, walking up behind Catarina and placing his hand on her shoulder.

Catarina shrugged off his hand and lowered herself back into the wheelchair. "Mind your own business!" she said, then swivelled around and wheeled toward the door.

"What did you say to her?" Angela asked.

"I told her that horse is crazy. He's dangerous, and you should stay away from him."

Angela reached out to Storm, and he moved slowly toward her. She turned to Tony. "Give me a few days with him before you remind Barazza to call Lorenzo, okay?"

"You girls are as crazy as that horse is," Tony scoffed, and left the stable.

If I can prove he's trustworthy, maybe Barazza will change his mind, Angela thought.

"What do you think, boy?" She approached Storm, speaking in a soft voice. Storm was small and would be easy to mount. "Would you let me on your back?" Storm turned his head toward the girl and pricked his ears forward. Angela reached out her hand. "I can ride you; I know I can."

Storm ignored her for a moment, and then tentatively stretched out his neck. He touched the tips of her fingers with his nose, then gave a quick snort and pulled his head back. He pawed the stall floor with his left front foot, bobbing his head up and down. "Okay, okay," Angela said, backing out of the stall and pulling the door closed. "But I'll be back."

She went into Bella's stall and pulled a bridle down from the iron hook. "Hello, girl," she said, stroking the mare's angular head. Bella was a lot taller than Storm, so Angela found a box in an empty stall to stand on while she slipped the bit into Bella's mouth. Then she pulled the bridle over her long ears, fastening the strap under her jaw.

The dapple moved up to his stall door, peered around the post and watched Angela.

She carried the box in one hand as she led the mare outside. But the box wasn't high enough for her to reach the mare's back, so she grasped a handful of coarse mane and pulled herself up onto Bella.

Angela felt as if she were on top of a mountain. She reined the mare around and headed toward the paddock, relishing the familiar feeling of happiness and contentment she always experienced on horseback. She clucked her tongue, and the mare broke into a jarring trot that chattered Angela's teeth. She clucked again, dug in her heels, and the mare launched into a cumbersome gallop. Bella was easy to exercise and responded to Angela's every command.

Half an hour later, Angela led Bella back into the stables and slipped off her back. Storm was waiting for them, his eyes bright and ears swivelling. His head hung over the stall door, his long grey-white mane cascading between his ears, partially obscuring his eyes. Angela thought he looked like one of those pretty carousel horses, the ones she'd loved riding at the summer fair when she was a girl.

Angela bridled Francesco next and took the broad-backed bay through his paces in the paddock without a saddle. He was spirited but responded to Angela's commands without hesitation. She raced him full out four times around the paddock, the distance to qualify for the Palio time trials. She was impressed by how smooth and fast he was, but she just knew Storm could beat him.

She thoroughly rubbed Francesco down and combed him. After making sure he had water and hay, she checked Storm's stall, then went into Bella's.

Tony entered the stables carrying a saddle that he hung over the railing of Bella's stall. "How'd you make out today?" he asked.

"Not bad," Angela said, smiling up at him. "I just finished."

"So you like the job? You'll stay?"

"I will."

Tony washed his hands in the bucket of water outside the stall.

"Are you practising for the Palio?" she asked.

"Yes, I'm going to ride for the Giraffe contrada." Tony smiled at her, his eyes flashing. He dried his hands on an old towel hanging from a nail. "I'm hoping they'll draw Gino, the small black." He ran his hands through his hair, and the curls sprang back, glossy in the light. "The Unicorns—Giorgio and Barazza's contrada—they could use a fast horse this time. They haven't won in years."

Angela dropped the curry-comb in the straw and picked up the brush, staring at its bristles thoughtfully. She drew the brush across Bella's knobbly ribs. "What about the dapple, Storm?"

Tony looked surprised. "What about him?"

"Couldn't he be entered in the Palio?"

Tony laughed. "The only entry that horse is going to make now is into the slaughterhouse." He walked over, cupped Angela's chin in his hand, leaned in and placed a gentle kiss on her surprised lips. "Forget about it, *amore mio*," he said softly, looking into her eyes. "You ready to go home? I'll give you a ride."

"Sure. Five minutes?" she said, feeling dazed.

"Great. I'll be at the house."

When Angela arrived home, Aunt Maria was serving a late lunch. "Angie, sit down and eat," she said, as she scooped ladles of steaming soup into a bowl and nodded toward a plate full of fresh buns, cold prosciutto and cheese. Angela was famished after the long morning at the allevamento.

"You like Tony?" Aunt Maria asked.

"Not really," Angela said, avoiding her aunt's gaze.

"You be careful of that boy." Aunt Maria narrowed her eyes and handed her niece a slice of cheese.

"We were talking about the Palio, that's all."

"You be careful of Tony," she repeated, tucking a strand of hair behind her ear, lowering her chin and wagging a finger at Angela. "He likes lotsa girls."

Aunt Maria's different than my mother, Angela thought. She liked her aunt and felt comfortable with her—she was outspoken and loud, but in a lovable way. Angela's aunt was the very opposite of Angela's mother, who kept her thoughts to herself.

"I met Catarina today."

Aunt Maria nodded. "Ah, she is a nice girl. Too bad about her accident."

"How long ago did it happen?"

"A few months." Maria's eyes clouded over. "She lose her mother the year before that."

Angela remembered when her dad had suddenly died of a heart attack. It was awful. One day he was there, and the next he was just gone, but his coat was still hanging behind the door. It was odd when everyone told her they were sorry. *What did they have to be sorry about?* She knew they meant well, but it sounded so stupid.

That night, Angela lay in bed thinking about the dapple. Her heart ached as she pictured him being loaded into a truck and taken away. He would be frightened, not knowing where he was going. And then when he got there...

She shuddered and pulled the covers up to her chin.

Chapter Three

Over the next couple of days, Angela went straight to Storm's stall with the hope that he hadn't been taken away. She was surprised to find him still there and thought that Barazza had forgotten his vow. Angela was careful not to frighten Storm and always brought a pocketful of treats to gain his trust. He soon began to whinny when she arrived and eagerly nuzzled her pocket.

In the meantime the gangly mare, Bella, had become an amusing companion. Angela was pleased to learn that the mare liked to jump, so she took the time to set up a course in a field that wasn't being used. For an hour each afternoon, she taught Bella how to jump over bars she had placed between two barrels, gradually raising them as Bella gained confidence.

Storm wasted no time in voicing his annoyance at being left out of all the fun. He whinnied loudly from inside the stable until Angela finally said, "Okay, but you have to let me put a lead on you."

As Angela approached Storm with the lead in her hand, his skin quivered and his eyes flashed. She secured the rope around his neck, led him to the field and slipped the rope off. At first, Storm watched from a distance. But soon his curiosity got the better of him and he galloped along beside them, veering off at the last second as Bella took the jumps. Often, even on the lowest jumps, Bella would hit the top bar and knock it off. Bella was no show horse, and they weren't competing, so Angela didn't mind. She was pleased to be jumping again.

One morning, Barazza wheeled Catarina's chair out onto the patio. Occasionally, when Angela glanced up, she could see Catarina watching. When Angela had finished taking Bella over the jumps, she walked over to talk to Catarina, who was listening to music on her iPod.

"Hi," Catarina said. Bella stretched out her neck and rubbed her nose on Catarina's shirt, leaving wet spots. Catarina laughed and pulled out her earphones. "You listen to music much?" she asked Angela, stroking Bella's nose.

Angela nodded. "My favourite band is the Honey Girls."

"The Honey Girls! I love them!"

"I went to their concert once with my friend. I had to tell my mom we were going to the movies." Angela made a face. "She never would have let me go."

"You saw them live? You're so lucky!" Catarina grinned. "I'd love to see them! Were they good?"

"They were awesome!"

"I used to dance around the room when I played them," Catarina said, closing her eyes and swaying her head. Suddenly, her smile disappeared, and she opened her eyes. "I guess I'll never dance again." She looked down at her leg, and then at Angela, who quickly looked away.

"Go ahead, say it!" Catarina said roughly.

"Say what?" Angela asked. She was amazed at the sudden change in the tone of Catarina's voice.

"It's ugly. Say it's ugly! I know you want to!"

"No, it's not ugly. It's...it's..." Angela looked into Catarina's eyes and wanted to be totally honest with her. She wanted to be her friend. "It's...it's ugly!" she said.

Catarina stared back, her eyes two pinpoints of black pain, her mouth set in a determined, grim line. This time Angela didn't look away. *She probably hates me now.*

Neither girl spoke, and then suddenly Catarina burst out laughing. For a moment Angela was silent, not knowing how to react, but Catarina's laugh was infectious. Soon Angela was laughing too. They laughed until the tears came.

"Want to go to my room and listen to the Honey Girls?" Catarina asked, between gulps of laughter. "I just got their latest CD."

"Sure," Angela said, wiping tears from the corners of her eyes. She tied Bella to the porch post. "Just for a bit, though. I have to put the horses away."

Angela followed Catarina as she wheeled the chair toward the house. Just then there was a loud ruckus in the paddock. They stopped and turned around to see what it was. Storm was bucking and kicking, whinnying loudly and racing around in circles.

"What the—" Angela said.

Storm reared up and struck the air wildly with his front feet, tossing his head violently.

"He's trampling something!" Angela gasped, clutching Catarina's arm.

"Oh no!" Catarina's hand flew to her open mouth. "Oh no!"

Angela bolted off the patio and through the paddock gate in an instant. "Easy, boy," she said soothingly. "Easy, boy." She stepped slowly toward the horse. Storm feebly pawed the ground with one front hoof, his whole body trembling, his energy spent. He had worked up a fierce sweat that glistened on his heaving sides. His head bobbed up and down; his long soft mane bounced.

"Shhh, it's all right now," Angela murmured as she grasped his halter. "Okay, boy, it's okay." She stroked his damp neck and spoke softly to him. She didn't want to look at the ground and see what he had trampled.

She glanced up at Catarina, who waited anxiously on the patio. Angela forced herself to walk over and look at the trampled object. She let out a sigh of relief and chuckled at what was left of a saddle blanket that had been hanging over the fence.

"It's just a blanket!" she called out to Catarina. "It must have slid off the fence and frightened him!" Angela picked up the blanket and placed it on the top railing again.

"Storm, you silly boy!" she said as she stroked his nose. "You mustn't spook so easily! What is it, huh? What has made you so afraid?"

Storm blew snorts of air against her shoulder as he nudged her with his nose. She led him out of the paddock to where Catarina waited on the patio, looking like she had just seen a ghost.

"Are you okay?" Angela asked.

Catarina nodded slowly. "Those sounds...they brought back memories," she said. "I...I think I'm okay now but..." She looked at Storm with concern. "Why do you suppose he does that?" she asked. "Just flips out like that?"

Angela shrugged. "Who knows? Must be something that sets him off. If we could just figure out what, we could help him!"

"Look at him," Catarina said, watching Storm chew on a clump of dry grass. "He's fine now!" She glanced at her watch. "I didn't realize it was so late. I have to go! My therapy session—it's at eleven." She grimaced. "I hate it! She's always telling me, 'now stand on that leg, Catie.' Hmmph! A lot she knows! *Her* legs are just fine!" She turned the wheelchair around toward the house. "We'll listen to the new CD when I get back!" she said.

"Catarina?" Angela asked.

"Uh-huh?" Catarina stopped the wheelchair and turned back.

"I'm going to take Storm for a ride after you leave. See if I can figure out what sets him off."

Catarina's face brightened. "Okay! I'll keep my father in town as long as I can, so he doesn't find out." Her face turned serious. "Be careful, though!"

"I will. C'mon, you two," Angela said to Storm and Bella, tugging at their halters. "Let's go back to the stable."

Angela put Bella back in her stall, then turned to Storm. "Okay. It's time to go for a ride. Are you going to trust me?"

Angela removed Storm's halter, grabbed a bridle and approached him, murmuring softly. Ever so carefully, she slid the metal bit between his teeth and slipped the headpiece over his ears. He didn't seem to mind. *So far, so good*, she thought. He chewed on the bit and studied her face. "See? That's not so bad, is it?" She rubbed his neck. "C'mon," she said, leading him out of the barn and into the paddock, glancing quickly around to be sure no one was watching.

She moved Storm a safe distance away from the paddock gate, slid one leg over his back and eased herself up, grasping a handful of thick mane. Immediately she felt his muscles bunch up beneath her. His tail swished, and he shifted from one foot to the other, crow-hopping sideways. His head bounced, and he blew a few quick, successive snorts to let her know he didn't like what she was doing.

Angela urged Storm into a gallop. He responded eagerly. Catarina was right—the horse could run. They raced around the paddock, a perfectly matched pair, horse and rider blended into one. Storm's rhythmic gallop was comforting, and Angela's body easily moulded to his. *How could they even think of destroying such a beautiful animal?*

The first lap around the paddock went smoothly enough. By the second lap, Angela began to relax. On their third pass, she felt the horse's muscles bunch up beneath her. Suddenly, Storm reared up and threw her. She flew through the air and slammed into the ground with a thud. When she blinked her eyes to clear her vision, she saw Storm standing nearby, his reins dangling in the dirt. A squirrel dashed into the nearby bushes, its tail twitching.

"Oh, no you don't, Storm. You're not getting off that easily," she said, dusting herself off and picking up his reins.

Angela searched for a grassy area that might soften her landings. The paddock ground was way too hard. She found what she was looking for in a field behind the stables. The grass was thick and lush underfoot, like a carpet. She could hear the sounds of a nearby river through the trees on the edge of the field. *The air is much cooler here*, she thought. "Okay, boy, I'm getting back on." She remounted Storm, who took several steps sideways, then relaxed as they rode to the edge of the field, following the sound of rushing water.

She dismounted and led Storm down a trail that crossed over the corner of the field into a stand of oak trees. As the trail emerged from the stand of oak, it narrowed and wound downhill toward the river, then twisted and turned as it followed the fast-moving water. There was little space to manoeuvre between the river and the bank that rose sharply upward. It was not a trail for the faint of heart; one slip and they could be whisked away by the rapid torrent below. An idea began to form in Angela's mind. It was a risky one, and if it failed, she didn't want to think of what might happen. Maybe she would bring Storm back and try it tomorrow.

"How'd it go?" Catarina asked when she saw Angela at the stables later that afternoon.

"Great! For a few minutes. Then—boom! A silly squirrel frightened him, and he dumped me on the ground."

Catarina groaned. "There's worse news," she said. "I overheard Papa talking on the phone. Storm's going to be picked up next week."

The news sliced through Angela like a knife. The two girls stared at one another, knowing they both felt the same.

"What are we going to do?" Angela asked.

Catarina shrugged, tears welling up in her eyes. "I don't know," she said. "I just don't know how to change Papa's mind."

Wordlessly, Angela headed toward Storm's stall, and Catarina followed. The dapple whinnied softly as the girls approached. He blinked through his long, silken mane. His eyes seemed bright and intelligent as he greeted them. Angela thought of what was going to happen and couldn't look at him.

"I don't know what happened that day," Catarina spoke quietly. "We were just riding on the trail at the edge of the field, and he reared up suddenly. The next thing I knew, I woke up in the hospital. The doctors said my leg injuries weren't just from the fall. Papa said Storm must have struck me with his hooves after he threw me, like he did with

the blanket. Papa said only a crazy horse would do that."
Catarina pulled the cuff of her sweater over her hand and
wiped the tears from her cheeks. "Maybe, but he doesn't
deserve to die." She turned to Angela. "We've got to do
something!"

Angela was quiet for a few minutes. "I have an idea," she
said. "It's a bit far-fetched, but it just might work."

Chapter Four

The next day, as the girls had planned, Catarina got her father to take her into town for the afternoon. That gave Angela time to carry out her plan and have Storm back in the stall before they arrived home.

"Okay, Storm," Angela said as she reined him toward the paddock gate. Bella plodded firmly after them. "Not this time, Bella. You can't come with us." She pulled the gate shut, and the mare reached her long neck over it, whinnying softly. Angela rubbed the velvet on her nose. "See you later, old gal."

Storm seemed in a good mood, and Angela had no trouble mounting him. They rode to the edge of the field and down onto the trail. Angela hoped that taking Storm along the narrow river path would force him to focus his attention and not be spooked so easily. But her plan was fraught with danger. The river was high, the current swift and the path treacherous. She steered Storm toward the river and nudged him with her heels. He seemed puzzled by the unfamiliar terrain, but when the smell of the water reached his nostrils he tossed his head, pricked his ears forward and quickened his step.

The trail narrowed at the bottom where it joined the riverbank. The river rushed by. On their right, the steep bank rose sharply upward, peppered with rocks, bushes and trees. Angela spoke to Storm over the sounds of the water. "Okay, boy. It's only you and me. Let's just take it easy."

Storm's ears flicked back as though he understood. With a quick and lively step, he picked his way over the stones that littered the narrow path. She could feel his excitement. The air was cool and fresh as they followed the crooked path along the river. Her plan was working. Storm appeared calm, intent and focused on the path ahead. Angela felt satisfied, but thought about turning back because it was getting late.

The sharp cry of a bird pierced the stillness, and a large hawk suddenly swooped down in front of them. Startled, Storm whinnied and reared, his front legs pawing the air. Angela clung to his long mane, trying to stay on, afraid of falling into the swiftly moving river directly below. But Storm's mane slipped through her fingers and she fell. Rocks scraped her back and branches tore at her clothes as she slid faster and faster down the bank. She hit the icy water and gasped in shock, sputtering for breath as the water covered her head. The frigid current twisted and churned, pulling her under. A sharp pain shot through her knee as it struck something hard. Panic spread through her. Her lungs felt as though they would burst. Frantically, she struggled toward the surface. As her head broke through, she gasped for air. Spying a thick branch hanging over the water, she grabbed it and pulled herself hand over hand toward the bank, finally dragging herself out of the water.

As she collapsed on the shore, she heard Storm's muffled whinny. "Storm!" she yelled, pulling herself up. "Storm!" She saw him struggling in the cold water about twenty feet downstream, fighting to keep his head above the surface. Terrified, he fixed his wild eyes on her, whinnying in distress. Angela limped down the narrow shore. "Storm! Hold on, Storm! I'm coming!"

She plunged back into the swift-moving water and swam toward him, fearing the current would pull her past him. She grabbed for his bridle and held fast as the water pulled them downstream. She slipped one arm around his neck and drew her body close to him as they plunged into the churning rapids. The river tossed them about like a cork until they came to a quiet pool and found the ground beneath their feet. Angela collapsed on the pebble beach, and Storm lunged up the bank beside her. His head hung down and he blew long jagged breaths from his nostrils. Water dripped from the end of his nose.

Shakily, Angela got to her feet and ran her hands over Storm's body, checking for injuries. Apart from a few scratches on his legs and one on his nose, he seemed to be fine. "Thank heavens you're all right, Storm," she said, resting her head against his neck.

She looked around and saw the remains of an old campfire littered with a few empty cans and bottles. "Come on," she said, wearily tugging on Storm's reins. "Let's see if we can find a path. There's got to be one around here somewhere."

Storm raised his head and gingerly followed her as she limped off past the campsite toward a narrow path at the edge of the woods. It twisted and turned up the bank until it broke out of the brush into a field lined with neat rows of olive trees. Angela stopped, trying to get her bearings. She wasn't sure how long they had been in the water or how far they were from Barazza's. Darkness was falling quickly, and the wind picked up, chilling her wet body. The evening sky glowed with an eerie light; storm clouds gathered, threatening rain. As Angela and Storm threaded their way through the olive trees, the first fat drops of rain began to pelt down. Angela shivered, moving closer to Storm for warmth. He nickered and rubbed his nose against her. Then, just in front of them in the gathering dusk, Angela could make out the outline of a fence. She mounted Storm and closed her eyes as he galloped along the fence back home to the allevamento.

Chapter Five

Angela slid off Storm's back outside the stable. A tall figure stood silhouetted against the bright security light mounted outside the building. As Angela squinted to get a better look, the figure moved forward.

"Angela?" Barazza called out. "Are you all right?"

"Yes!" Angela called back.

Barazza walked toward her, and Angela saw Tony behind him.

"Thank God! What happened?" Barazza asked.

"Storm got spooked by a hawk. We fell in the river, but we're okay."

"Are you crazy? I told you that horse is dangerous! What were you doing riding him?" Barazza asked angrily as he grabbed the reins from Angela and held them out to Tony. "Take him back to the stable."

As Tony reached for the reins, Storm's ears flattened back against his head. He reared up, striking the air with his hooves. Barazza grabbed Angela and pulled her away, as Tony took the reins and tried to calm the horse. Terrified, Storm's head twisted from side to side trying to break free. Pulling away from Barazza's grasp, Angela ran to Storm and snatched the reins from Tony's hands.

"No!" she cried. "He's frightened! Can't you see? Let me take him. He trusts me." She reached out and stroked the trembling horse. Storm stood still now, his sides heaving, his nostrils snorting puffs of steam in the damp air. "It's okay, Storm," Angela murmured in a soothing voice. "It's okay." She ignored the worried faces of the two men and led Storm past them into the stable.

Once Angela had rubbed Storm dry, settled him into his stall and given him clean hay and water, she returned to the house. Tony was sitting at the kitchen table. Barazza was making coffee, banging the cups and saucers, his forehead creased in a frown. Catarina sat quietly in her wheelchair, and the girls exchanged glances.

"I have called your aunt and uncle to let them know you're all right," Barazza said, as he rummaged through the cupboards. "Where are those biscuits? I can never find the biscuits in this house!" He slammed the cupboard shut. "Tomorrow, we'll get rid of that horse. I'll call Lorenzo first thing in the morning to come and get him. Tony, make sure you're here before eight to help load him into Lorenzo's trailer."

Barazza's words sent a chill through Angela. "No, please, Mr. Barazza," she pleaded.

"You're shivering," Barazza said, handing her a towel. "Maybe Catarina has something you can put on." He nodded at Catarina. "Catie?" he said.

Catarina tipped her head toward the bedroom, motioning Angela to follow.

Tony glanced at his watch. "I'd better be going. I'll see you in the morning," he said.

As soon as Angela had closed the door behind her, Catarina spun the wheelchair around and faced her. "What happened?" she asked anxiously.

Angela slumped on the edge of the bed and stared at her hands. "A hawk swooped down and spooked him." She looked up. "Catarina?"

But Catarina wasn't listening. She was looking right through Angela. "A hawk," she said quietly to herself.

Angela nodded.

"A hawk!" Catarina exclaimed. Her eyes focused with a sudden realization. "That's what happened the day of my accident!" She pushed her chair closer to Angela and leaned forward. "A hawk flew up on the side of us! I remember now! That's what happened. It was the hawk that must have frightened him!"

"But that doesn't make sense," Angela said. "He's seen birds fly in front of him before, and it hasn't bothered him."

"Wait a minute, what about the blanket?"

Angela's eyes widened, and she grabbed Catarina's hand. "And the squirrel in the paddock...that's it!" she exclaimed. "That's it!"

"What?" Catarina asked.

"What side of Storm did the hawk fly up on?"

Catarina shut her eyes tight and was silent for a moment. "I think...I think it was..." She opened her eyes, looking apologetic. "Oh Angie, I can't remember!"

"Think, Catarina, think hard! It could save Storm's life."

Catarina shut her eyes again, and Angela waited for what seemed like an eternity. The silence was unbearable.

Finally, Catarina opened her eyes, and Angela saw the sheen of tears. "It's all just a blur. I...I just remembered there was a hawk. I remember it shrieking, but I don't know what side it was on." She searched Angela's face. "I can't remember, Angie, I'm sorry!"

"It's all right," Angela said, consoling her.

"What are you thinking?" Catarina asked.

Angela jumped up and paced the room, her hands thrust deep into the pockets of her wet pants. "There was a horse at the stables back home—a jumper—his name was Calibre. He was a gentle, easygoing buckskin, but he always shied at a particular jump and nobody could figure out why. This jump, it was an easy one, not too high, but it had a big basket of flowers hanging at one end. Then someone suggested it might be the pot of flowers that bothered him. So we had the vet examine his eyes, and you know what?" She turned to Catarina. "He was partially blind in one eye! Nobody had noticed it before. The flower pot was hanging there, but he couldn't make out clearly what it was, so it spooked him."

"So what does that mean?" Catarina asked.

"The saddle blanket fell on Storm's right side. And the day he dumped me in the paddock, the squirrel ran out on his right side!"

"Do you think that could be Storm's problem too?"

"I'm sure of it! I'll bet it's Storm's right eye!"

"Then we can get the vet to look at him!" Catarina said. Her face beamed with joy. "Angie, you're a genius!"

Angela grimaced. "Yeah, sure," she said. "Now we just have to convince your father before it's too late." She turned to the door.

"No, wait!" Catarina said. "Not tonight. He's tired and grumpy. He was really annoyed about you riding down by the river. Let's tell him first thing tomorrow morning."

"NO! The man is coming from the slaughterhouse! We have to tell him *now*!"

Catarina shook her head. "Lorenzo won't be here early. He's never on time for anything. Trust me, Angela, I know my papa. It's better if we tell him in the morning."

"But how will I get out here that early?"

"Why don't you just sleep over? I'll have Papa call your uncle. Now come on, get out of those wet clothes, and let's get something to eat!" She pulled open a drawer and handed her a pair of silk pyjamas. "And you can call me Cat," she said, over her shoulder.

Later, Angela brushed out her damp hair as Catarina manoeuvred herself into her pyjamas.

"So, how are you gonna convince Papa that Storm is blind in one eye?" Catarina asked.

"I'll ride Storm in the paddock, and you wait by the fence on our right side and spook him with a scarf when we pass."

"But he'll throw you!" Catarina said.

"That's the idea! He has to freak out, or your father won't believe us."

"But what if he hurts you? Like...like he did with me."

"Don't worry, he hasn't yet." Angela put down the hairbrush.

"Ange?" Catarina asked.

"Yeah?"

"Do you like Tony?"

Angela turned toward Catarina, surprised. "Sure, I think he's cute. Why?"

"Be careful, okay?"

Angela laughed. "We're not dating each other, if that's what you mean."

"I know; just be careful, that's all."

"Okay," Angela said with a smile.

Chapter Six

The next morning, when Angela and Catarina emerged from the house, the first few rays of light could be seen in the sky. It promised to be a beautiful day.

"Morning, girls," Barazza said, leading Storm out of the stable. "You're up bright and early." He pushed his floppy hat back, smiled and scratched his head.

Neither girl spoke, and Angela looked at Catarina, unsure who was going to start the conversation.

"Did you sleep okay, Angie?" Barazza asked.

Catarina looked at Angela, then back at her father. "Angela has an idea. I mean, about what might be the matter with Storm."

"I think he might be partially blind in one eye, his right eye," Angela said.

"Blind?" Barazza said, chuckling. "This horse isn't blind. Where did you girls get that idea?" He turned and looked at Storm's eye and frowned.

"We can show you," Angela said.

"How are you going to do that?" Barazza asked.

"Let me ride him and I'll show you," Angela said. She dashed into the stable without waiting for a reply and returned with Storm's bridle.

Barazza handed Angela the lead rope and folded his arms across his thick chest. "This I have to see."

The little dapple pushed his velvety muzzle against Angela's shirt and nickered as she removed his halter and slid the bridle up over his ears. She reached her arms around his neck, revelling in his softness. "C'mon, Storm," Angela said, tugging on his reins.

Storm stretched out his neck, tossed his mane, and stepped lightly after her. Catarina pushed her wheelchair behind them as they moved toward the paddock.

Before she reached the gate, Angela stopped and waited until Catarina was beside her. Angela reached out and gently tugged the orange scarf from Catarina's hair. "Here." Angela handed it to her. "Let us ride by you twice, then on the third round, suddenly wave the scarf. But wait until he's almost alongside you, so he won't see it with both eyes."

Angela put on a brave face, but her stomach danced with butterflies. It was one thing to talk about being thrown, but to actually plan it? That was crazy! She just hoped she could roll out of the way in time to escape Storm's wild hooves. She remembered how he had pulverized the blanket, and goosebumps covered her arms. "C'mon, boy," she murmured to Storm.

Once inside the paddock, Angela pulled herself up onto Storm's back and watched Catarina roll toward the fence, the orange scarf tucked tightly in her lap. Barazza followed behind with a worried expression.

Angela nudged Storm with her heels, and he broke into a gentle trot. She prodded him again, and he rocked into an easy canter. They headed around the paddock and made their first pass by Catarina, who nodded. Storm cantered on, oblivious to their plan. Angela's mouth felt dry. Her stomach clenched as she rode by Catarina a second time. Angela grasped the reins firmly and tightened her knees, though she knew it wasn't going to help her stay on Storm's back if he really wanted to throw her. As they rounded the bend a third time, she watched Catarina's hand close around her scarf. Storm's gentle canter brought them closer... closer...closer. Suddenly Angela saw the orange scarf fly up and flutter. Storm's muscles bunched beneath her and his front legs left the ground. Angela felt herself sliding sideways and heard Storm's frightened whinny. In an instant, she thudded onto the ground, and a jarring pain stabbed her shoulder.

She saw Storm's soft grey underbelly above, his legs frantically flailing. She tried to roll, but pain jolted through her injured shoulder. Desperately, she scrambled to her hands and knees.

"Angela!"

She heard Catarina's scream.

"My God, he's going to trample her!" Barazza shouted.

Angela scurried out from underneath Storm and didn't turn around until she knew she was clear. She wiped the dirt out of her eyes and cleared her vision. Storm pawed the ground with one front hoof, his head bouncing, his nostrils snorting like a steam engine, his skin trembling.

"Easy, boy," she murmured. "Easy."

Barazza burst through the gate as Angela stood on her shaky legs and gingerly felt her shoulder.

"For God's sake, girl! Are you all right?" Barazza reached out to steady Angela.

"I'm all right." Angela said. "It's his right eye!"

"*Mamma mia!*" Barazza exclaimed. "Such a crazy way to show me!" Barazza looked over at Storm, who stood with his head hanging, his energy spent. "All right, all right," he said, looking back at the girls, "I'll have Umberto check out his vision."

Impulsively, Angela planted a quick kiss on Barazza's stubbly cheek. But she winced with pain as she drew away.

"You're hurt!" Barazza said. "We should drive you in to the clinic."

"It's nothing," Angela said, gritting her teeth. "I'm okay. I'd better put Storm away."

"You'll be black and blue tomorrow," Catarina said, "and stiff! You'll need to take it easy."

"Hmmph!" Barazza said. "Her? Take it easy? Is like telling a bird not to fly!"

Angela picked up Storm's reins. "I know, boy," she said. "I'm sorry. But I had to do that. Now you get to stay!" Storm bounced his head up and down, and Angela and Catarina laughed.

"Come up to the house when you're done, and I'll get you an ice pack," Barazza said.

"The girls are right, Cesare," Dr. Santini said in English, turning to Barazza. "The vision in Storm's right eye is impaired. But he's not blind. Any sudden movement on his right side would startle him." Dr. Santini snapped his rounded leather bag shut and stood up. He patted Storm's neck.

"Thanks, Umberto," Barazza said, shaking the vet's outstretched hand.

"You could put a blinker on the right side of his bridle. Would probably take care of the problem," Dr. Santini offered. "Or even try an eye patch. They don't usually take to those too well, though," he added.

Angela couldn't hide her delight or her smug grin. "Oh, Cat," she said, as she watched Barazza walk Dr. Santini back to his van. "Isn't that the best news ever? Storm can stay! You can ride him again!"

"*Me?*" Catarina exclaimed.

"Well, yeah," Angela said. "You want to ride him, don't you?"

"I guess…"

"You can ride him when your leg gets better," Angela said.

"I can't!" Catarina protested.

"Sure you can! I'll help you!"

Catarina vehemently shook her head. "Nuh-uh. No way."

"Cat!"

"No way."

"I'll help you. You can even start on Bella."

"No!" Catarina pushed her wheelchair toward the house.

"Cat! Wait!" Angela shouted, quickly tying Storm's reins to the post and running after her. "Cat!" She reached Catarina's chair and grabbed hold of it, turning her around. "Cat, listen!"

"No, I can't!" she said, tears falling down her cheeks.

"You just have to sit on the horse. You can do that! You're doing it right now."

"I can't!"

"You're scared of falling," Angela said sharply.

"I am not!"

"You're scared!"

"No!"

"Yes, you are, Cat. But it's okay. I understand. You think I'm not scared lots of times? Think I'm not scared to death before every competition? You think I wasn't scared out there today?"

Catarina sniffed again, wiped her nose on her sleeve and looked up. "You were?" she said. Her eyes were flooded with tears. "It didn't seem like it. I thought you were so brave."

"I was terrified! I felt like throwing up!" Angela leaned closer to Catarina. "You've gotta do it, Cat! You've gotta get on again!"

"I can't," Catarina whispered.

Angela knelt beside the chair and looked up at her friend. "I'll help you, Cat. It'll be okay, I promise. Besides, Storm likes you."

Catarina shook her head.

Chapter Seven

The blinker was such a simple little device, but it worked. They attached a circular piece of leather to the bridle near Storm's right eye, blocking his vision on that side. Storm had been wearing it for two days and didn't seem to mind it.

Now that Storm's life was no longer in danger, Angela and Catarina talked about getting him into the Palio. But first, they had to find a way to get Storm into the selection line-up for the time trials, and there were only a few more days left.

Angela headed into the barn, silently practising how she could approach Barazza.

"Mr. Barazza, do you think Storm could..."

"Mr. Barazza, about the line-up for the time trials..."

"*Mr. Barazza, Catarina and I thought that Storm might...*"

She pictured him throwing up his hands the way he did when he was exasperated. Angela sighed and felt in her pocket for the special treat she'd brought for Storm. She'd snaffled sugar cubes from the coffee counter at the bakery, carefully avoiding Aunt Maria's watchful eyes. Storm sniffed them out the moment she entered his stall, his velvety lips nibbling at her pocket.

"I knew you'd find them." She rubbed the patch of hair between his eyes and planted a kiss on his nose. "And we'll find some way to get you into the Palio." Her arms circled his neck, and she pressed her face into the tangle of his mane. She suddenly realized how much she would miss him when she returned home. Storm pushed his nose against her, sniffing and blowing softly.

"I'm jealous."

Angela spun around at the sound of Tony's voice. He grinned at her as he leaned one hip on the entrance post of the stall. His snug white T-shirt was tucked neatly into his black jeans. She pushed the hair out of her eyes and smiled at him.

"I haven't seen you for the last few days," she said. "Where have you been?" She wanted to say she'd missed him, but she saved it.

"I've been riding one of the horses at the Cerillo allevamento for the Giraffe contrada. He's in the line-up for the time trials," he said, entering the stall. "I watched you and that crazy horse race around the paddock yesterday. You're quite a rider."

"He's not crazy; he's a great horse. He's just partially blind in one eye, but the blinker has taken care of that. I think he's ready to run in the Palio."

"He's too unpredictable. Anyway, the line-up for the trials has already been chosen." Tony stepped closer to her, brushing a loose strand of hair back from her forehead. "You have beautiful eyes, Angie," he whispered, leaning into her. He trailed his finger along the line of her jaw and brought it to rest on her lips. Then he pulled her into his arms. Angela felt flushed as his lips brushed softly over hers. "Come on, finish up here, and I'll take you for dinner."

Tony took her to a small trattoria on the edge of town where he knew the owners. The waitress rushed up to hug him, glancing sideways at Angela. Tony slipped one arm around Angela's waist and steered her to a table nestled in the corner. He held her hand across the table and ordered pizza.

Angela reached into her pocket, turned her cellphone off, smiled at Tony and asked, "Can't we put Storm in the line-up in place of Francesco?"

"I don't think Emilio would go for that. Francesco ran last year and did very well."

"Who's Emilio?"

"He's the official who runs the trials."

"But why can't he also time Storm? It's just four laps around the paddock. Storm is sure to beat Francesco."

"It's not as simple as that. Emilio has timed over thirty horses from *allevamenti* all over Tuscany. Tomorrow's the last day. Maybe next year."

"But I won't be here next year!"

"Okay, okay, *amore mio*." He smiled, squeezing her hand. "Emilio's timing Monticello, a horse I'm riding at the Cerillo's tomorrow. I'll talk to him. He's coming to Barazza's to time Francesco afterwards."

"Who's riding Francesco?" Angela asked with a startled look.

"Fabrizio. Haven't you met him yet?"

Angela shook her head.

"He's the jockey the Unicorn contrada hired this year," Tony continued. "He'll ride Francesco through all the time trials, but not necessarily in the Palio because each of the winning trial horses goes into a draw to match them with a contrada. Each contrada hires their own jockey."

The waitress brought the pizza and smiled at Tony. He served Angela a slice and took one for himself.

Angela smiled. "So if Storm wins in the time trial, he would be in the Palio."

"Sì."

"And if you convince Emilio to get him into the line-up tomorrow..."

"Sì, sì, I'll do what I can."

Angela reached over and squeezed his hand.

After the meal, he drove to a small field and parked. The stars were perfect, and the light of a quarter moon drifted in and out of the scattered clouds. Tony pulled Angela close and kissed her, long and deep, his free hand cradling her cheek. Shivers ran down her spine. She had never been kissed like this by the boys back home. Their kisses had been fleeting, furtive and inexperienced—never like this. This was real. But Tony's kisses grew stronger and more demanding, his hands searching. *No! Not like this!* she thought. She grabbed his hand, pushing it away. "No, no, Tony. I can't!" she whispered. "I can't!"

"It's all right," he whispered softly. "It's all right." He reached his hand under her shirt and swiftly unhooked her bra.

She struggled upright and pulled away, straightening her clothes and refastening her bra. "It's late. Take me home. My aunt will be worried."

Tony sighed. "Very well."

He was quiet on the drive home. He pulled up in front of the bakery and turned to her.

"I will call you tomorrow, sì?"

"Sì." Angela leaned over and kissed him. "Don't forget to talk to Emilio about Storm."

"Sì." He smiled and drove off.

The kitchen light burned brightly as Angela walked up to the bakery. She straightened her shirt and walked through the door. Aunt Maria sat at the table, a cup of coffee in her hand.

"Why did you turn your cellphone off?" she asked. "I tried to reach you."

Angela smiled guiltily. "Sorry, Auntie, I forgot to turn it back on after exercising the horses."

"I told you watch out for that Tony," Aunt Maria said, raising one eyebrow.

"Sì," Angela answered. "I'm fine, honest."

Chapter Eight

The next day Angela brought Storm into the paddock. She was anxious to see how fast he could run the four laps. She brought Bella out so the mare could watch. Bella rested her bony chin on the railing and waited.

The air was warm. A slight mist rose from the nearby valleys, encasing the sun in a feathery haze. Angela breathed in deeply. She leaned forward and stroked Storm's neck, pressed her knees into his sides and urged him into a gallop. She felt the wind in her hair and the fresh air on her face. She rode bareback, imagining them riding in the Palio, feeling the movement of every warm muscle beneath her. Her body rose and fell with the horse's rhythm.

"Go, Storm," she whispered, as if they were pulling ahead of the other horses, riding like the wind. "We can do it. We can!" Storm galloped faster and faster around the paddock. His pounding gait and the wind whipping her face took Angela's breath away. She closed her eyes and clung to his sides with her knees. She was mesmerized by Storm's speed.

Suddenly, Angela heard the thundering hooves of another horse bearing down on her. She turned and saw Francesco, his neck outstretched and nostrils flared, pulling alongside her. She saw the narrow-boned face of the tall, skinny rider and knew he must be Fabrizio.

Angela dug her heels into Storm, urged him forward, and he responded, surging ahead. Rising to the challenge, Fabrizio whipped Francesco, trying to catch up with her. But Storm held the lead as they raced around the paddock— once, twice, three times—then his gallop gradually eased into a gentle canter. Fabrizio slowed Francesco and pulled up beside her.

"Beginner's luck," he scoffed.

Angela ignored him, reining Storm to a slow walk. She leaned forward and stroked the horse's sweat-soaked neck. "Wow!" she said to Storm. "That was some ride." He swivelled his ears back, listening to her words, his breath coming long and full, steaming in the morning light.

Angela walked Storm around the paddock to cool him down. She slid off his warm, moist back and stood in front of him, holding his head between her hands. She pressed her face into the soft crevice of his neck. Storm blinked at her and blew through his nostrils, then pushed his nose into her shoulder, almost knocking her off balance. She laughed. "We'll get into the Palio. I know we will!" She looped his reins over the fence post.

"Angie!"

Angela turned and saw Catarina coming toward the paddock, an excited look on her face.

"Angie!" Catarina pushed her wheelchair up to the paddock gate. "Emilio's here! He saw everything!"

Angela's heart thumped. She looked up and saw Barazza coming toward them, followed by a short, stocky man.

Emilio was staring at Storm. "Is this the crazy horse?" he asked, turning to Barazza, who nodded. Emilio thoughtfully stroked his chin. He had a narrow moustache, bushy eyebrows and a stomach that extended far out over his belt. He jerked his head at Storm. "Should I time him too?"

Barazza nodded. "Sì."

Angela quickly hugged Storm. "Can I ride him?" she asked Barazza excitedly.

Fabrizio stepped up beside Barazza. "I'll ride him."

Angela looked at Barazza hopefully.

"Angela can ride him," Catarina spoke up quickly. "She's a good horsewoman."

Fabrizio mumbled something in Italian and scowled at her.

"Sì, go ahead," Barazza nodded at Angela.

Catarina gave Angela a grin and a thumbs-up sign.

Chapter Nine

Emilio stood at the paddock fence, stopwatch in hand, with Barazza and Catarina beside him. Angela took a few deep breaths to quell the butterflies in her stomach. Storm sensed her anxiety and crow-hopped. She spoke soothingly to him. "Easy, boy. It's only four laps."

Angela reined him over to the fence, took another deep breath and looked down at Emilio. The chunky man simply nodded. He tipped his head toward the paddock, motioning for Angela to begin the run.

"You go, girl!" Catarina grinned.

Angela turned Storm and walked him onto the track. She leaned low over his neck and ran her hands down his shoulders. "Show them what you can do, Storm," she said softly, then nodded at Emilio.

She pressed her heels into Storm, and he took off in a burst of speed. He had never run this fast with her before.

She clung with her legs, wrapped her hands in his mane and leaned low over his body. The figures outside the fence flashed by in a blur. She was amazed at how fast they completed the first lap. Storm's hooves drummed the ground. The second lap seemed even faster. *Only two more,* she thought. Storm stretched out his neck and continued to fly around the track. She heard Catarina and Barazza cheering as they completed the final lap.

Angela slowed Storm to a walk, then reined him in near the fence and slid off his back.

Storm stood still, his head down, sides heaving. Angela stroked his sweaty neck. She hugged him. "You were great!" She led him back to the gate and was surprised to see Tony. He pulled it open to let them pass. Fabrizio rode Francesco past them into the paddock, stopped and waited for Emilio's signal to begin.

Tony smiled and put his arm around Angela's shoulder. "Storm made great time! Better than my trial with Monticello."

"That's fabulous!" Angela said.

She smiled at Catarina, who raised her hand in a high-five. "You did it, Angie!" she said, wheeling up to them.

"Not just me, Cat. I couldn't have done it without your help!" Angela hugged her and turned to watch Francesco. "Let's see what Francesco's time is."

Emilio nodded his head, and Fabrizio kicked his heels into Francesco's sides and struck him with the whip.

Francesco took off around the track, Fabrizio whipping him every step of the way. When he'd completed the final lap, Francesco was soaked with sweat and foam dripped from his mouth. Fabrizio reined him in and jumped off.

"Good ride," Barazza said. He looked over at Emilio, who was shaking his head.

"Not good enough," he said. "We'll take the dapple."

Angela turned and threw her arms around Tony. He quickly kissed her on the cheek. "Sorry, I gotta run. I just stopped by to watch."

As he walked away Angela turned to Catarina. "Isn't this great?"

"Yeah." Catarina forced a smile. "Sure." She turned and watched Tony get into his car. A frown creased her forehead.

"Mamma mia! What you feed that horse, Cesare? Gunpowder?" Emilio slapped Barazza on the back and reached out to shake his hand. "See you at the time trials. Eight o'clock sharp tomorrow morning. Good luck!"

"So?" Catarina asked, eyeing Angela. "Something going on between you and Tony?"

"I've been meaning to tell you." Angela blushed. "I just haven't had a chance. It's nothing really. He just took me out for dinner the other night."

"Did he try anything?" Catarina asked.

"Well, no, not really. I mean, sort of. But I stopped him. He took me home when I asked him to."

Catarina was silent for a moment. Then she leaned back in her chair. "You have to be careful of Tony. I've known him a long time. He's not what you think he is."

"What do you mean?"

Catarina looked at her and smiled. "Just be careful, that's all. Don't get taken in by him."

Angela shrugged.

Later that night as Angela lay in bed, trying to sleep, Catarina's words kept swirling in her mind.

Chapter Ten

The next morning Angela bathed Storm with a bucket of warm water and soap, lathering his tail and mane and scrubbing his back and legs thoroughly. Then she combed his dappled coat until it shone. She pulled his halter off the hook and slipped it on. "Today you're going for a ride in the trailer," she whispered in his ear. "Then you're going to run in the trials. And if you do well, you'll be in the Palio!"

Storm bounced his head up and down, and pushed his nose against her, anxious to get out of the stall. He strained against the door. "Okay, okay!" she chuckled. "We're going right away!"

Angela led Storm outside and breathed in the morning air. The sun poked its rays through the tops of the trees, turning the Tuscan soil red. Angela loved it here.

"I won't be riding you today, but I'll be there cheering you on. You've got to show them how fast you are, that you can run like lightning, no matter who is riding you. You mustn't throw Fabrizio. Promise me, Storm, promise me you'll be good!"

Storm nickered a soft reply.

Angela longed to be the one to climb on his back and ride him in the trials, but she knew it was out of the question. Women jockeys didn't ride in the Palio.

Once Storm was loaded into the trailer for transport to the trials, Angela dashed up to the house to talk to Catarina. She knocked on the big wooden door, but no one answered. She checked her watch and cursed under her breath. *The driver will be here any minute.* She ran around to Catarina's bedroom window and tapped on the glass. After a few moments, the curtains parted and a sleepy-eyed Catarina peered out. Angela waved and Catarina motioned for her to come in. Angela let herself in the front door and made her way to Catarina's bedroom.

"Cat! I'm so excited! I can hardly wait. Wish us luck!"

Catarina sat up in bed and grasped Angela's hands. "Storm's going to make it. I know he is!"

"I've got to run," Angela said, giving her a quick hug. "Will you be coming soon?"

"Yes! I wouldn't miss it for the world! Papa will drive me in." She looked at the clock on the bedside table. "I'd better get dressed." She threw back the covers, swung her legs out, grasped the table edge and pulled herself up.

"Do you need some help?" Angela asked.

"No thanks. I've been practising!"

As Angela climbed into the front seat of the big truck that pulled the long trailer carrying Storm, the driver grinned at her. "That grey," he said, in halting English. "Everybody say he going to win."

"He will!" Angela smiled back. "Just you watch. He will!"

Once they got to the track, Angela helped the driver unload Storm and made sure he was comfortable. Just then Catarina and Barazza pulled up.

"Look, Angie," Catarina said. Grasping her father's hand, she pulled herself out of the car. She wobbled for a moment then took several hesitant steps forward, supported by her father. Her face glowed. "I can do ten steps now!"

"That's fabulous!" Angela hugged her. "Pretty soon you'll be riding!"

Catarina made a face. "I don't know about that!"

Barazza took out the wheelchair, and Catarina sat down in it. A few minutes later, Fabrizio appeared. His eyes lingered on Angela. Storm snorted, threw his head up and backed away.

"Easy boy," Angela murmured.

Fabrizio grabbed the reins tightly right underneath Storm's chin. Storm pulled backward, but Fabrizio jerked Storm's head down and quickly mounted his bare back. Storm crow-hopped sideways, and Fabrizio roughly reined him in.

Angela exchanged glances with Catarina who frowned.

"Be gentle with him," Angela said.

"I know how to handle horses," Fabrizio answered. He dug his heels in and headed Storm toward the starting line.

Angela, Catarina and Barazza pushed through the throng of anxious spectators, weaving their way through the crowd toward Giorgio, who had found a good viewing spot close to the track.

The trials were very informal so the jockeys jostled each other for position on a first-come, first-served basis. Any horse that got the inside track was just lucky. Storm ended up in the middle of the pack, behind a long rope that served as the start line. The Palio officials stood nearby and were only interested in the horse's speed and time. It didn't even matter if the jockey fell off, as long as the horse finished the course.

When the rope dropped and the horses thundered forward, Storm burst into the lead. Tony, astride a strong dark bay, was right behind, in second place. Angela felt the excitement of the crowd and the drumming of the hooves in the soil beneath her feet. As Storm pulled ahead of the others with ease, her heart filled with pride. But Fabrizio heeled Storm hard, and the horse's ears swivelled back. Storm's right front leg buckled under him and he stumbled, struggling to regain his balance.

Several horses gained on them as the dapple found his footing again. Storm recovered his stride, but as the other horses galloped past, Fabrizio struck his whip repeatedly against Storm's side.

Angela saw the horse stiffen, saw his ears go back, saw Fabrizio fly through the air and land with a thud in the orange-brown soil. Storm tossed his head as he picked up speed again and raced off to catch up with the others. In no time at all, he came abreast of the lead horse, and with the finish only a few lengths away, stretched out his neck, summoned one more burst of speed and crossed the line in the lead. The crowd roared.

Angela pushed through the milling throng, making her way to the finish line, followed by Barazza, Giorgio and Catarina. Two men tried to grab Storm's reins, but he avoided them, dancing from side to side and throwing his head up in the air.

Angela hurried toward Storm and reached for his reins. The horse was skittish, fear still in his eyes, and he bounced his head a few times before allowing her to take the reins.

She ran her hand over his nose, then down the length of his sweat-soaked neck, reassuring him with soft words.

Fabrizio angrily strode up and grabbed the reins from Angela. *"Stupido cavallo, ti mostrerò io chi è il capo!"*

Storm reared, and Barazza suddenly stepped up and took the reins from Fabrizio. *"Lascialo da solo!"* Barazza shouted. *"Ci penso io."*

Fabrizio cursed and stomped off.

"Take it easy, boy," Angela said as she slipped her arm around Storm's neck and took the reins from Barazza's outstretched hand.

Storm nudged his nose into her shoulder and snorted softly.

"What did they say?" Angela whispered to Catarina who had wheeled up beside them.

"Fabrizio called Storm a stupid horse and said he would show him who's boss. But Papa told Fabrizio to leave Storm alone."

Angela saw Tony handing the bay's reins over to a groom nearby. As Tony wiped the back of his neck with his scarf, she tried to catch his attention. "Tony!" she called, but he continued walking away from her, and her voice was lost in the crowd. She turned to Catarina and asked, "How did Tony's horse place?"

"I think he was third," she said, turning her attention to Storm. "You were great, Storm," she said, pushing herself up from her wheelchair. She steadied herself and reached out her hand. Storm nickered and nuzzled her palm.

Angela waited anxiously as one of the race officials, a tall thin man with a hooked nose, walked up. His face was composed and serious. He spoke with Barazza in a low tone.

After the official left, Barazza glanced at Angela, nodded and grinned, giving her a thumbs-up. Catarina clapped her hands with excitement, and Angela threw her arms around Storm.

"You're in the Palio! You did it!" Angela exclaimed. She pulled Storm over beside Giorgio and Barazza. "When is the draw to match each horse with a contrada?" she asked.

"Wednesday," Giorgio said. "We have a chance, Angie, a great chance of winning if we draw Storm."

Chapter Eleven

Angela was just beginning to understand the intricacies of the Palio. It was much more than a horse race. It was all about honour and pride, and often the passionate desire to win made people forget about the welfare of the animals involved. It was not uncommon for a horse to be badly injured, and Angela wondered how pride in a tradition could be so important that the life of an animal could be disregarded.

The town hummed with talk of the race. Hordes of tourists arrived. Some were lucky enough to rent prime viewing spots on balconies overlooking the Piazza del Campo for a small fortune.

"It's all about tradition!" Giorgio laughed as he and Angela walked up to the entrance of the Unicorn contrada's building. "Our contrada's roots are centuries old. This is our symbol. See? *Leocorno*, Italian for unicorn," he said, pointing to the elaborately carved unicorn plaque outside the entrance. "This is where our horse will be stabled."

Young boys and girls stood in circles practising tossing flags. They twirled the flags and threw them high in the air over their heads, attempting to catch the handles as they fell. Giorgio nodded toward a man dressed in medieval attire of orange tights, blue and white velvet cape and hat, hurling a banner high into the air above his head. Other men carried flags depicting the mascots of their *contrade*: Giraffe, Porcupine, Dragon, Owl, Eagle, Tortoise, Goose, Caterpillar, She-wolf, Shell, Wave, Panther, Forest, Tower, Ram, and Snail.

"When a child is born into a family in Siena, they are also born into a contrada," Giorgio said. "We tie a pink or blue ribbon to our flags. When a member dies, we drape the flags with black crepe. We are all family, and the Palio is our most important event." He smiled at Angela. "We prepare for it all year with suppers and bingos to raise enough money to pay for a good jockey. You must pay well to secure a good one."

"Did Barazza choose Fabrizio?" Angela asked.

"No, our contrada officials chose him. He's a good jockey. If we draw a slow horse, we might make a little deal, huh?" He leaned in and said in a low voice. "*Partiti.*" He rubbed the fingers and thumb of his right hand together. "We maybe switch jockeys with one of our allied contrade, so they can win. Then they'll owe us a favour."

Angela and Giorgio waded into the crowd, jostling for space amid men in colourful tights waving their banners and drunken locals, arm in arm, singing the praises of their contrada.

"Hang on to my arm!" Giorgio yelled as they headed up the street and stopped in front of a church with massive wooden doors, surrounded by an arch adorned with cherubs and lambs. "On the day of the race, we have a magnificent parade. The men dress in colourful velvets, silks and brocades, just like today, only even fancier. The horses are dressed in finery too, and our horse will be taken right inside this church to be blessed before the race."

He turned to Angela. "We will draw Storm, and he will win, no?" But Angela didn't answer. "Sure he will!" he said, patting her shoulder.

Angela hoped he was right. As they walked through the Piazza on their way back, she envisioned the horses hurtling around the square, circling it three times in ninety electrifying seconds, dust flying from their hooves, riders airborne above their bare backs, risking life and limb for the honour of winning the Palio banner. Angela shivered.

Chapter Twelve

The next day, Wednesday, was the day of the draw, three days before the Palio. Barazza, Fabrizio, Angela, Catarina, Giorgio and Maria stood together in the midst of the crowd to see which horse their contrada would draw. There was a wooden platform erected in the centre of the Piazza. The platform held two steel cylinders on stands, one at each end. Several race officials stood in between the cylinders, and one of the officials held a microphone. While one official drew a slip of paper bearing a horse's name from one cylinder, another official drew the name of a contrada from the other. The names were then passed to the man with the microphone, who announced the match.

The crowd was feverish, pushing and shoving in an attempt to get closer to the front. Three burly-looking men guarded the barricades to hold the crowd back. As each pairing was read aloud, another man posted them on a board in letters large enough for everyone to see.

Loud cheers greeted some of the announcements; emotional jeering, booing and swearing greeted others. Angela strained to hear Storm's proper name, *Tempesta*, above the roar of the crowd. Butterflies churned inside her. She looked down and realized she was clenching her fists. She unclenched them and placed a hand on Catarina's shoulder. Angela's mouth felt dry. She squeezed her eyes shut. *Storm, Storm, please let us get Storm!*

Then she heard the announcer say in a loud voice, "Tempesta." She waited, holding her breath, for him to read out the match. Seconds ticked by slowly.

Then, suddenly, his voice boomed out, "Leocorno."

There was a mix of cheers and boos from the crowd.

"That's us!" Angela shouted and grabbed Catarina's chair, spinning it in circles. "Uncle Giorgio, that's our contrada! That's the Unicorns! We get Storm!" She bounced with excitement; Maria was screaming; Giorgio was crying and laughing and crossing himself. Catarina was yelling, "Yes, yes, yes!"

Barazza pounded Giorgio on the back. "This year we will win for sure!"

Angela scanned the sea of faces in the crowd looking for Tony. She hadn't seen him since the trials, and she couldn't find him now. When she turned back, Fabrizio was looking down on her, his skinny body outlined by the late afternoon sunlight, thin hair sprouting from the top of his narrow head. She thought he resembled a rooster or perhaps a rabbit, noticing his two jutting front teeth.

"I guess you are happy about the draw, no?" Fabrizio asked. "That horse he is fast, very fast. But a little nasty." He sneered. "Nothing that can't be taken out of him, eh?" He hitched up his pants with both hands, fingering his belt. "No horse throws me twice. I'll soon beat it out of him. Leave it to me."

Repulsed, Angela stepped away from him. As she turned back toward Catarina and the others, Angela heard his deep low chuckle. "Never met a horse I could not control," he called after her.

Angela shuddered and wished Tony were riding Storm. Tony would be good to him.

Just then a stooped, grizzled old man with thick white hair walked over, picked up Storm's lead rope and led him away.

"Where's the old man taking Storm?" Angela shouted in Catarina's ear, leaning over the wheelchair.

"To our *stella*, our stable," Catarina shouted back. "That's Libby, our *barbaresco*, our horse handler. Libby will watch Storm twenty-four hours a day."

Barazza, Angela, Catarina, Giorgio and Maria joined the throng of excited contrada members as they fell in behind

Libby and Storm. Men were arm in arm, singing the horse's praises and chanting, "Tempesta, Tempesta, Tempesta."

The stable was made of stone, had high, arched ceilings, a cot, a table and chairs and an attached feed room. Storm's stall was at the back. A thick bed of clean straw awaited him, and an intricately woven gold and blue blanket hung over the stall door.

Giorgio motioned to the cot. "Libby will even *sleep* here with Storm," he said to Angela. He leaned over and lowered his voice. "Libby looks forward to this all year. He likes to get a break from his wife, Carmen."

Maria swatted Giorgio's arm. He chuckled, straightened up and spoke louder so Libby could hear. "Libby's wife, Carmen, holds the honoured position of flag-maker and mender for our contrada. For forty-six years she has sewn, mended, ironed and looked after the beautiful coloured flags you see being twirled by our members. It is a year-round job!" He grinned. "Eh, Libby?"

Libby, bent over inspecting Storm's front hoof, snorted at Giorgio and returned to his work. Giorgio laughed, put his arm around Angela and kissed her cheek.

"Storm will stay here until after the race," Barazza said. "We need to protect him from jealous rivals and keep a close watch on him. Don't worry. He will be pampered and well cared for until the race is over. The contrada's honour depends on this horse."

"Maria and I go back to the bakery," Giorgio said to Angela. "You can stay with Storm until he is settled." He patted her shoulder. "Are you okay to walk home alone?"

"Sure, it's only a few blocks," Angela answered.

Barazza and Catarina turned to go.

"Mr. Barazza?" Angela asked. "Have you seen Tony today?"

"Ah, yes!" Barazza said. "You did not see him? He was at the draw, to listen for his mount." He frowned. "He will ride Gino, the small black who won last year, a formidable opponent for our Storm. It will be a close race!"

After everyone had left except for Angela, Libby washed and brushed Storm until his coat shone. "A fine, fine horse," Libby said in English as he ran his gnarled brown fingers down Storm's legs. He turned to Angela. "This is a special one. I feel it in my fingers. These legs carry magic."

Angela was happy to see that Storm had taken a liking to Libby too. He nuzzled Libby affectionately whenever the old man passed within reach. Angela liked Libby and returned to the bakery satisfied that Storm was in capable hands.

Chapter Thirteen

Later that afternoon, Angela joined a crowd that had gathered to watch several young men practise the flag-twirling. She was overwhelmed by the sense of excitement throughout the small city, which had risen to fever pitch as the countdown to the race began. The flags were large, more than four feet by ten, yet they were handled like small batons, twirled and tossed high in the air, sometimes passing beneath a leg, an arm or around the back. Angela was amazed at the men's dexterity.

"They begin practising when they are only three or four years old, you know," Angela heard a voice say as a hand rested on her shoulder. She turned and looked into Tony's eyes. He squeezed her shoulder. "Would you like to go out for dinner?"

Angela loved the way Tony cocked his head to one side when he asked a question. "Sure," she said with a smile. "I'd love to." She looped her arm through his as they walked to his car. "Tony?" She turned to him as he slid into the seat next to her.

"Mm-hmm?" He pulled out into the traffic.

"I wish you were riding Storm for us."

"Sì, that would have been perfect."

"Do you think you could talk to Fabrizio? You know, about not being so hard on Storm?"

Tony didn't answer.

"Please. Maybe he'll listen to you," she continued.

"Sure," Tony said, taking her hand. "I'll talk to him."

Angela felt better, but inside she was worried. If Fabrizio couldn't understand how to handle Storm, they would never be able to win.

Tony drove them to a small restaurant tucked away in an alley between two tall buildings. Angela sat opposite him at a round wrought iron table. The waitress seemed to know Tony well, just like the waitress at the other restaurant had. She flashed her eyes at him, and he smiled back at her.

"What would you like, Angela?" Tony asked, opening the menu.

"You choose."

"You're on." He grinned, closed the menu and called the waitress over.

The waitress came by and took their order, fussing over Tony. She seemed to think Angela was invisible. When the waitress had left, Tony reached over and covered Angela's hand with his. "You're very special to me, Angela. I really like you."

Angela's voice softened. "I really like you too, Tony."

"I will be very busy the next few days. We ride every morning and evening in the pre-race trials to familiarize the horses with the treacherous course. The sixth and final trial is on the morning of the Palio. We won't be able to see much of each other."

"But you will talk to Fabrizio?"

"*Sì, sì, amore mio.* Don't worry."

Later, when they'd finished eating, they sat holding hands and talking until the restaurant owner, a short squat man, cleared their table and hustled them away.

"C'mon," Tony said, grabbing her hand. "I'll take you to a special place."

The open convertible sped around tight hairpin curves as it climbed above the city. Angela could see the lights of the buildings below. Tony reached over and stroked her knee. "Isn't it beautiful?" he asked. Angela smiled and nodded.

Soon the lights were nothing more than twinkling dots as they left them far behind. Tony slowed the car and pulled onto a bumpy side road. The headlights rested on an old church as Tony brought the car to a stop and switched off the engine. Angela leaned her head back against Tony's arm. The sky above her was a mesmerizing blanket of twinkling stars.

"Mama used to bring me up here on picnics," Tony said. "We'd sit in that grassy field next to the church. While she fixed lunch, I would climb up the old church steeple and ring the bell. From the top I could see forever. Then she would yell at me to come down, but I would lean over the edge and tease her until she threatened to tell Papa."

Tony turned and pulled her close. Angela closed her eyes. She felt like the whole world had gone away and there was just the two of them. She pushed her face gently into the curve of his neck.

Tony lifted her chin with one finger and kissed her.

His hand ran over the swell of her breast, down to the curve of her waist, over her hips and along the outside of her thigh. Angela felt herself giving in. She pulled away from him.

"I'll race you to the church," she said, opening the door. "C'mon!"

She hopped out of the car and ran toward the church. Its facade glowed softly in the moonlight. Behind her she heard Tony's footsteps. Just before she reached the church, she felt his hand grab her waist.

"Gotcha!" he said, spinning her toward him and pulling her down onto the grass.

"No!" she shrieked, laughing. He rolled on top of her, the weight of his body pinning her to the ground. He pulled her hands over her head and held them. As her laughter subsided, he lowered his lips onto hers. She felt the warmth of his kiss and the weight of his body pressing into hers. It felt good. He moved his hands down her body. Angela relaxed and gave in to his gentle persistence. *"He's not what you think he is,"* Catarina's voice echoed inside Angela's head.

Angela turned her face away. "No, Tony, no!" She placed her hands under his chest and pushed him away.

Tony rolled over onto his back, rested his arm across his forehead, stared at the stars and sighed.

"Maybe you'd better take me home," she said, sitting up and smoothing her clothes.

"Sì," Tony said, getting up. "I'm riding early in the morning, anyway."

Chapter Fourteen

"What is it, Uncle?" Angela asked Giorgio the next day as he hung up the phone, frowning and shaking his head. "Is everything okay with Storm?"

"That was Libby. Storm threw Fabrizio again in the pre-race trial this morning. That's twice in the last two days, and Libby is worried." Giorgio checked his watch. "It's almost time for the *Prova Generale*, the trial race tonight."

"I'm going to the stable to see Storm," Angela said, grabbing her jacket and backpack from the hook beside the door.

"We'll see you later at the banquet," Giorgio said. "Libby will know where our table is."

She hurried from the bakery to the Leocorno stable. The cobblestones under her feet were damp and shiny. As she passed the Piazza she noticed that the early evening's gloomy drizzle had dampened the rich soil that had been trucked in to cover the race course. It was no longer dusty. She pulled her jacket together at the front to shut out the damp air, and adjusted her backpack.

If only I could ride Storm. Angela was deep in thought as she rounded the corner and entered the stable. She heard several nervous whinnies and wondered if Storm was bothered by the mice. Yesterday, he had created a fuss about the mice scuttling around his feet. What the stable needed was a few cats. But as she walked toward Storm's stall, she heard a rustling sound that was too loud for mice. Storm began stamping his feet and snorting.

Angela saw the back of a man's head appear above the stall door, but she couldn't make out who it was. "Libby?" she called, hurrying.

Suddenly, Storm reared up, striking the air madly. The man inside the stall threw up his arms, but Storm struck him with his front hooves, knocking him down. There was a horrible scream as Storm brought his hooves down repeatedly, trampling the man.

Angela flung open the stall door and saw Fabrizio writhing in pain, clutching his bloody right leg.

"Easy, boy," she said soothingly, stepping slowly toward Storm. "Easy, boy."

Storm's head bounced up and down and the whites of his eyes flashed as she moved him away from Fabrizio. Storm stamped his hooves and his skin quivered, but he gradually calmed down. Angela heard Fabrizio curse. Suddenly, Libby was behind her, dragging Fabrizio out of the stall.

Storm stared wide-eyed at Angela as she ran her hands over his body, checking for any injuries. She couldn't find anything wrong, but when she bent over to check his hooves, her eye caught sight of something half-buried in the straw in the corner of his stall.

She reached down to pick it up and gasped. It was a syringe. She looked closely at its murky yellow contents. It was half full. Angela turned her attention to Libby, who was just closing his cellphone. Fabrizio lay moaning on the cold stone floor.

"Ambulance coming. Tempesta, is he all right?"

"Storm's okay, just frightened, but I found this," Angela said, holding out the syringe.

"*Mamma mia!*" Libby said, crossing himself.

Chapter Fifteen

D r. Santini stood next to Storm and stroked his neck. Giorgio and Barazza had arrived. "I've checked him over completely and taken some blood samples," the vet said. "I'll give the blood and the syringe to the lab, and we should know in a couple of hours if Storm was injected." Dr. Santini placed the blood-filled vials and the wrapped syringe inside his bag. "Do you want to report this to the police, Cesare?"

"No, Fabrizio got his punishment."

"But he was trying to drug Storm!" Angela exclaimed.

Giorgio put an arm around his niece. "This sort of thing happens. When a contrada doesn't get a good horse, they try to make things difficult for an enemy contrada who has a better horse. Or they will help an allied contrada win. Maybe Fabrizio make partiti with a rival contrada."

"I never liked Fabrizio," Angela said. "And Storm didn't like him either."

Then the realization suddenly hit her. *We don't have a jockey! Now we won't be able to run in the Palio tomorrow!*

Barazza saw the look of disappointment flooding her face. "Yes," he said, reading her thoughts. "We cannot run in the race now."

Angela was crushed. By now, Storm had missed the evening trial. And all the available jockeys had already been chosen for the Palio. All of the wheeling and dealing and trading was finished. All of her dreams for Storm had vanished in the blink of an eye—all because of a stupid jockey. She hated Fabrizio. *He's lucky Storm didn't kill him.*

She tried to hide her disappointment but couldn't. All the feelings she had bottled up over the last few weeks burst inside her, and she began to sob. She dropped into a chair and cradled her head in her hands.

Giorgio came over to comfort her, rubbing her shoulder. "It is all right, Angela. There's always next year."

"I won't be here next year," Angela wailed. "I won't be here!"

"Angie, don't be so upset." Giorgio placed his arm around her.

"I can't help it. I wanted so badly to see Storm in the Palio—to prove to everyone that he is a good horse."

"There may be another way," Barazza said rubbing his chin thoughtfully.

"How?" Angela sniffed, looking up at him.

"We still have time to find another jockey. The deadline is tomorrow morning, after the *Provaccia*—the final trial race."

"Where can we ever find another jockey at this late hour, eh?" Giorgio scoffed. "Even if we can find one, we have to pay him a fortune." He threw up his hands. "We cannot afford this!" He paced back and forth in front of Angela. "We leave it to next year. Next year we choose a good jockey. We will win."

Barazza spoke quietly. "Next year we may not draw this horse. This is our chance to bring home the banner. Tempesta, he is the fastest horse I have ever seen. It is our good fortune to draw him this year."

"Aacchh!" Giorgio said. "It is the will of the Virgin Mary. She will give us this horse next year too."

Barazza shook his head. "No! We cannot take that chance. This is our time to win—we must grasp it." He slammed his fist in his hand. "We *have* another jockey."

"Who?" Giorgio asked. "The jockeys register tomorrow! And what about the banquet? It's about to start, and Fabrizio is supposed to make a speech."

"I'll take care of it," Barazza said. "Don't say anything to anyone. The celebration must go on."

Chapter Sixteen

The streets were crowded with pre-race revellers as Angela, Giorgio and Barazza made their way to the "good luck" banquet. Each contrada had blocked the streets with long tables covered in white tablecloths, surrounded by enough chairs to seat hundreds.

Numerous bottles of wine lined the tables, and candles flickered amid the brightly coloured centrepieces. The air was alive with shouting and chatter. Lights were strung along the fronts of the buildings to illuminate the banquet and everyone exuberantly waved flags supporting their contrada. Brightly coloured scarves bearing the symbols of their contrada adorned the heads of young girls or were wrapped around the waists of middle-aged ladies.

Down at the end of the street, Angela saw Tony's car.

"I'll be back in a moment," Angela said, as she moved away from the others. She noticed someone in the car with Tony and hurried toward it, calling out. But as she drew closer, the car pulled away.

She turned back to the banquet tables and spied Catarina waving a blue and orange Unicorn scarf matching the one twisted loosely around her neck. She motioned for Angela to come over, and Catarina tied the scarf around her neck. "See?" she said. "You are one of us, a member of our contrada!"

"I just saw Tony's car," Angela said, adjusting the scarf.

Catarina frowned, grabbed Angela's arm and pulled her down into a chair next to her. "You're not still crazy about him, are you?" she whispered. "Forget about him. He's no good."

"Why do you always say that?"

"He's got his hooks into you, hasn't he? You're not thinking straight."

"He has not! And I am thinking straight!" She glared at Catarina. "Why are you against him? What's he done to you?"

Catarina bristled at the question. "Nothing," she answered, turning away.

The banquet was a lively affair, and the more wine that was consumed the livelier it became. Women bustled about refilling plates and bringing more bottles of wine. Children danced around the tables, chasing one another with squeals of delight. Men swayed back and forth and sang loudly.

Catarina leaned over and nudged Angela. "We need to talk."

"What do you mean?" Angela asked.

"We need to talk about Tony."

Angela sighed and pulled back.

"No," Catarina said, grabbing her arm. "You have to listen to what I have to say!" Catarina leaned closer. "I had a relationship with him."

"You?"

"Yes, but Papa doesn't know about it, and he can't know about it!"

"Why are you telling me this, Cat?"

"Because I know how charming he can be and how much pressure he puts on, and how hard it is to resist him! He thinks he can get exactly what he wants." Catarina looked into Angela's eyes. "Don't give in to him! Once you do, he'll dump you. He won't be interested anymore, he'll move on to his next victim."

"How do you know?"

"Because I slept with him and he dumped me, just before my accident."

Angela's heart lurched. She wanted to go home, back to Canada. It was all too much. Storm wouldn't be racing in the Palio. And to top it all off, Catarina and Tony had been lovers! She wanted to escape from all this tension and just climb into her own bed and hide under the covers.

"Angie, talk to me," Catarina said.

"I don't know what to say," Angela replied. "I just feel kind of drained."

Barazza jumped up, went to the head table, grasped the microphone and addressed the crowd in Italian.

"Omigod!" Catarina exclaimed, turning to Angela.

The crowd suddenly became agitated.

"What's he saying?" Angela asked.

"Fabrizio has been injured!"

"I know."

"You knew about this? Why didn't you tell me?"

"Your father told me not to tell anyone. What's he saying now?"

"That we have another jockey, but he won't say who. Do you know?"

"No, I don't." Angela shrugged.

"C'mon, Angie."

"Honest, I don't know who it is."

Chapter Seventeen

"**M**e?" Angela looked up at Barazza in astonishment. She had been cleaning off the tables and helping to tidy up after the banquet. "You want me to ride Storm in the Palio?"

"You can't mean it!" Maria shouted, looking at Barazza incredulously. "It is a dangerous race! You know that. *Dio mio!* She's a little girl. *Mamma mia!* Where is your head?"

"We have no one else," Barazza replied. "If we drop out now it will bring shame on Leocorno, and Civetta—the Owls—they will laugh at us. They may even win."

"It is too risky," Giorgio said, shaking his head. "No, no, to ask a girl to ride in a man's race? I won't allow it. This is not just any race, Barazza. This is the Palio! The jockeys have to be tough. They have to be strong! She won't have the strength to hang on in those corners. And Storm, he is still unpredictable."

"That's just it," Barazza said. "The horse knows her. He behaves for her. Together they could win."

"Ah, Barazza! *Siete pazzo?* Are you crazy?" Maria said, throwing up her hands. "You are thinking crazy!" She paced back and forth.

"Do it, Angela." Catarina spoke quietly.

All eyes turned to the slim figure in the wheelchair. Catarina was staring intently at Angela. "Do it," Catarina continued. "There hasn't been a female rider in the Palio since Rosanna Bonelli rode for the Eagle contrada in 1957."

"Yes," Giorgio said. "And she fell at the San Martino curve! Remember? I tell you, it is too dangerous!"

Angela looked at Catarina, whose eyes seemed to dare Angela. She thought of how it felt to be on Storm's back, to feel his incredible strength beneath her. He was fast. She knew better than anybody just how fast he was. She knew he was capable of winning. She took a deep breath. "Catarina," Angela said, "I'll do it on one condition."

"What?" Catarina asked.

"If you agree to ride again before I leave."

"Angela, I don't care about your bargains," Giorgio said loudly. "I won't allow you to ride in this race."

"But, Uncle Giorgio, it's the only way," Angela said, turning toward him. "Mr. Barazza's right. I can do it. I've raced the obstacle courses at home. I'm an experienced show jumper; I can do it."

Giorgio groaned. "You don't understand. You have not seen this race. It is torturous!"

Angela turned to Catarina. "Will you?" she asked. "Will you ride again?"

Catarina stared back at Angela. The girls' eyes locked together, each one daring the other. Catarina didn't blink. She breathed deeply and spoke in a firm voice. "All right, I will," she said.

Angela turned back to Giorgio. "Please, Uncle Giorgio? Please let me. If we win, Unicorn will go down in history! The proudest contrada of all!"

Giorgio sat and dropped his head into his hands. "You are like your mother," he said in a muffled voice. "So stubborn. So impossible."

Angela rushed over to him and knelt in front of him, grasping his hands. "So you'll let me? You'll call Mom and tell her?"

Giorgio raised his head. "God forgive us," he said, "should anything happen to you."

Chapter Eighteen

Groups of teenagers bearing flags from rival contrade exchanged rude insults as Giorgio, Maria and Angela walked home. Young men broke into boisterous songs of self-praise and insults to their enemies.

Once in her bed, Angela found it difficult to sleep.

Fear had crept in. *What if I fall like Giorgio says? This course is treacherous. I could be killed.* She tossed and turned, pulling at the blankets and changing position every few minutes. Frustrated, she rose, pulled on a pair of sweats and a T-shirt and went outside.

She walked the few blocks to the Piazza del Campo, thinking about Tony. She felt torn between her feelings for him and Catarina's warnings. Deep inside, she knew Catarina was telling the truth, but Angela didn't *want* to believe it, and that was the problem. Catarina was right;

he *did* have his hooks into her, but she had more important things to worry about now.

The streets were still alive, humming with activity. A few scuffles had broken out near the track, but the police were on hand to break them up. Angela watched men and women as they dismantled the long banquet tables, rolling the stained white tablecloths into balls. The racecourse was littered with cigarette butts, empty bottles and the occasional discarded flag.

Angela stepped onto the course and gazed the length of one side, where it sloped downward into the dangerous and notorious San Martino curve.

Tony had told her that in all the history of the Palio, rarely had a race been run in which a jockey or horse had not fallen prey to the San Martino. Angela felt confident that Storm could cling to that curve. But could she stay on? She was relieved that the barriers had been padded with mattresses. She continued to walk the course and wondered what Tony would say when he discovered she was racing against him.

She reached the second notorious curve, the Casato, at the entrance to the Via del Casato di Sotto. Slightly less steep and sloping upward, it was nevertheless a formidable corner.

As Angela left the track and headed back toward the bakery, Tony's car slowly rounded the corner at the end of the street and stopped. Angela hid in the shadows and watched as Tony stepped out of the car and opened the passenger door. He drew a tall girl out and held her close, kissing her passionately. Then they both disappeared inside a building. Angela felt sick. *What a fool I've been!*

Numbly she stumbled back to the bakery, thankful no one was awake. She undressed and crawled beneath the covers, burning with anger. When at last she fell into a fitful sleep, she was plagued by dreams of the race. She was falling, falling, at the San Martino curve, with Tony standing over her, laughing.

"Angela, Angela, wake up!" Maria called from downstairs.

Angela bolted up. "Okay, Auntie, I'll be down in a sec."

"How did you sleep?" Giorgio asked as Angela entered the kitchen.

"Fine," Angela lied.

"Good, you have a big day ahead of you." He glanced at the image of the Virgin Mary and crossed himself. "May she keep you safe."

Aunt Maria placed a bowl of fresh fruit and a sweet bun on the table and motioned for Angela to sit. "Coffee is coming. Eat."

"I tried calling your mother last night," Giorgio said, "and I left a message for her to call back."

"A girl riding in the Palio, hah!" Maria cuffed Giorgio on the side of the head. "What were you thinking, huh?"

"I don't care what my mother says..."

"Don't worry, I'll convince her to let you ride."

Angela shook her head in disbelief.

"How will you manage that?"

Giorgio's hand fluttered dismissively. "You don't worry about that. You just make sure you stay on the horse."

After Angela finished eating her breakfast, Barazza arrived. "I've spoken with Dr. Santini," he said. "Storm's blood tests are fine. The syringe contained a sedative to make him sluggish, but Storm wasn't injected."

"I'm going to the hospital," Giorgio said. "I have questions for Fabrizio."

"Come, Angela," Barazza said, checking his watch. "We must get ready for the Provaccia."

The Provaccia, or bad trial, was the final practice run before the Palio. But it was not really a race; it was just for show, because no jockey with any sense would run his mount hard on the morning of the big race. Nevertheless, Angela looked forward to the Provaccia, since it would give her a dry run on the course and a rehearsal of what the actual race would be like.

Outside, the city was already alive. It was as if no one had slept. Traces of the previous night's revelry still cluttered the streets, and bleary-eyed men hustled about setting up chairs and bringing televisions outdoors so those that didn't want to stand in the crowded Piazza del Campo, or couldn't afford tickets for the terrace or bleachers, could watch the race on TV.

In the centre of the Piazza, the souvenir stalls and umbrella-shaded café tables were pushed back for the more than 75,000 expected spectators, including foreign and Italian tourists, who had come to Siena to see the race. Those who were unable to secure a position in the surrounding balconies or bleachers had already begun filing into the oval to watch the race standing up.

The cloud cover was thin, and it looked as though the day would prove to be a scorcher. Angela made a mental note to drink lots of water.

Storm was delighted to see her when she arrived at the stable, and whinnied his usual high-pitched greeting. Angela rubbed his nose affectionately. "Now it's just you and me," she whispered in his ear, scratching it softly. "You're going to be good for me, right?" Storm pushed his nose against her and snorted gently.

Angela helped Libby wash Storm and brush his dappled coat. She was so anxious, her hands were shaking.

"Word has spread to the other contrade that we have changed jockeys," Barazza told her. "But they don't know who our new jockey is."

That made Angela feel even more nervous.

"At eight o'clock we will attend a special mass led by the Archbishop. He will invoke the protection of the Madonna for the jockeys and their mounts. Here, you must put on these." He handed Angela a tunic and pants decorated with the bright orange, white and cobalt-blue colours of the Unicorn contrada. "This should fit. It is from last year's jockey. He was about your size. Carmen was up early this morning preparing it for you."

Angela took the silks from him and draped them over her arm. "Have you talked to Tony?" she asked.

"Ah, yes," Barazza answered. "But I didn't tell him you're riding for us." He raised his eyebrows. "You are very fond of him, eh?"

"No, he's just a friend."

Barazza shook his head and chuckled as she disappeared into the feed room to change. When she emerged, Giorgio had joined Libby and Barazza. They beamed when they saw her.

"Ah, my Angela," Giorgio said. "You are the finest-looking jockey we have ever had. Leocorno will be proud."

Angela blushed. She felt strange in jockey silks. "What did you find out from Fabrizio?" she asked.

"He admitted he made partiti, but he won't say which contrada."

"What's going to happen to him?" Angela asked.

"We don't pay him, and we never hire him again," Barazza answered.

Libby led Storm from his stall. "We will meet you at the Piazza after mass," he said.

The large bell of the Mangia Tower was tolling as Angela, Barazza and Giorgio made their way up the street to the church. She was thankful for her short hair, and had slicked it behind her ears, using Giorgio's hair cream. She hoped no one would notice she was a girl and was grateful for the loose jockey tunic that hid her breasts. Still, curious onlookers stared at her, trying to see who the new jockey was.

The light was dim inside the church. Lots of candles were burning, and the smell of incense filled the air. The Archbishop droned on.

Angela pictured the start of the race. Nine of the horses would line up at the starting rope in pre-assigned order, and the tenth horse, called the *rincorso*, would stay back from the line-up. This tenth horse would get a running start from behind, and the starting rope would drop when that horse reached the other nine.

Libby met them at the Piazza with Storm. As Angela mounted the dapple, Libby gave her some last-minute instructions and warnings for the Provaccia. She pulled on the helmet Libby handed her and moved Storm toward the starting position.

Storm danced on his feet as Angela reined him into position on the line. At the other end, she saw Tony astride the small black. She ducked her head, and a voice beside her growled something in Italian that sounded nasty. Angela looked up into the sneering face of a jockey who sat atop a tall black gelding in the position next to her. She couldn't be sure, but she thought he wore the colours of the Owl contrada, Leocorno's enemy. *Great!* she thought. *Of all the nine other contrade, I end up beside this one.* The jockey snarled again, looking Angela up and down with an expression of disgust on his face, then laughed.

The rope in front of them suddenly dropped. Storm surged forward. The crowd shouted and cheered as Storm pulled into the lead. Angela was breathless. Suddenly, she remembered that he needed to conserve his energy for the evening race. She pulled on Storm's reins, trying to get him to slow down, but he would have no part of it. He raced on, ignoring her attempts to slow him. Angela clung with her legs as Storm slid into the San Martino curve. It was sharp, sloping steeply to one side, and lived up to its legend. Storm flew around it on the inside, inches from the crowd pushing against the barricades. He maintained the lead, his neck outstretched, entering into the second lap.

"Storm! Storm! Slow down!" Angela yelled over the din of thundering hooves and the noise of the crowd. But he stayed in the lead around the third lap. Storm finished several lengths ahead of the others, amid the crowd's laughter and cheers.

Angela was elated that Storm had won, but she knew the others thought she was foolish and had probably squandered her mount's energy. She hoped they were wrong.

Libby met her at the finish line, his stubbled face grinning from ear to ear. He hugged Angela and took Storm's reins. "Ah, such a beautiful race, no?" he said.

"But I couldn't slow him down," Angela answered. "I shouldn't have let him run so fast. He'll be tired for tonight's race."

"Not this one," Libby said, stroking Storm's neck, a look of admiration on his face. "He has lots of strength to run again and again. You'll see."

Uncle Giorgio rushed over and gave her a hug. "You did a great job!" he shouted.

Then she heard Barazza say, "You make Leocorno proud. Now come, we must go to City Hall for the official signing of the jockeys. I tell you exactly what's going to happen while we walk."

Angela fell into step beside them, swivelling her head to see where Tony had gone.

She removed her helmet, then remembering her hair, glanced around her, spat on her hands and slicked it behind her ears.

Angela entered the City Hall ahead of Giorgio and Barazza. There were four jockeys already there when she walked in. A couple were chatting. She kept her head low and nodded to each one. As she was taking her place against the far wall, the door swung open and several more jockeys filed in, their richly coloured costumes lighting up the room like a circus parade. Among them was the sneering jockey from the Owl contrada. Angela kept her head low, not wanting to look in his direction. He was busy chatting with the jockey next to him. Angela held her breath.

"Angela!" It was Tony, grabbing her by the elbow and pulling her out of line.

She turned and looked into Tony's puzzled face. He stood staring at her, looking down at her silks. "Angela?" he said again, frowning at her. "You're the replacement jockey?"

"Yes!"

"You can't ride in this race!" He scowled at her. "You do, and we are finished!"

"You're making partiti with me?" Angela scoffed.

"Yes."

"I saw you with that girl last night."

"You were spying on me?"

"You're not worth the time. Let go of me!"

"She's an old girlfriend. She means nothing to me," he said, releasing her arm.

Just then the jockeys were summoned, and the mayor opened a large, ornately decorated leather-bound book for the signing of the contract.

When Owl's jockey stepped forward to sign, Angela stole a look at him from behind. He was broad-shouldered, like Tony, but not quite as tall. He wore his straight black hair in a ponytail tightly fastened at the back of his neck. It was heavily laden with hair gel and had a wet sheen to it. He moved with an air of confidence that unnerved her, and she felt her heart beat faster. Then the jockey in front of Angela took the pen and signed his name. The mayor's assistant passed the pen to Angela. She stepped forward, took the pen from his hand and with a defiant look at Tony, signed *Angela Carruthers* with a flourish. She handed the pen back, stealing a look at the assistant's face, but the man merely nodded and moved on.

Angela watched as Tony stepped up and signed his name. *I have to beat him! I have to win!* She looked over at Giorgio standing next to the contrada officials, and he casually glanced from side to side, then winked at her. She felt better.

The jockeys were presented with jackets bearing the colours of their contrada. Each contrada's *priore*, or captain, slapped his jockey on the back when it was all done. Giorgio nodded to Angela and did the same. He was trying to look very relaxed, but Angela guessed that he was as nervous as she was. As they milled around the room, Giorgio and Barazza were ushered aside by an official-looking man with a bushy, dark-brown handlebar moustache that sprouted out from the sides of his fleshy face. Angela watched them out of the corner of her eye. As the man kept pointing at her, Angela's stomach clenched into a knot. *Are they going to disqualify us?*

She tried to look inconspicuous among the group of jockeys, but her eyes kept returning to the three men. Another jockey elbowed her in the side, and she glanced over at him. "*Buona fortuna, eh?*" he said, smiling. He was a slight man with long fine fingers and slender arms. He wore the colours of the Tortoise, a contrada that Giorgio had told her was the Unicorn's ally. Angela smiled nervously.

She glanced over at the trio by the wall. They were still talking, their hands flying in all directions. *It doesn't look good*, she thought. If she were disqualified, it would mean the Unicorns could not participate in the race. There was no changing jockeys once they had signed their names. *And the shame!* Angela didn't want to think of the shame it would bring to the Unicorns to be disqualified for running a female jockey.

Giorgio and Barazza walked toward her. Angela shut her eyes. *Here goes.* She steeled herself, but Giorgio didn't say a word. He just took her arm and steered her toward the door.

Much fanfare greeted the jockeys as they emerged from the building. Angela ducked her head and stuck close to Giorgio and Barazza as they made their way past the crowd. When they were safely out of earshot of any officials or jockeys, Angela asked, "What did they say?"

"They know you're a girl. Signore Bonelli from the Giraffe contrada made an objection," Giorgio answered.

Tony! That rat! Angela thought.

"But the officials denied that objection because girls have raced before."

"Then the Owls complained because we changed jockeys so late," Barazza added. "They said we should be disqualified. But the rules say it's okay to change before the jockeys sign."

"The Owls are afraid because they saw how fast you ran this morning." Giorgio leaned toward Angela. "They are afraid they will lose! And you know what else? I find out they bribe Fabrizio to go to San Martino."

"What do you mean, Uncle?"

"They pay him to fall off at San Martino curve so we lose the race! That was the partiti he made. Maybe he decide himself to drug our horse to make sure he stay on to San Martino curve!" Giorgio laughed, straightened up and shook his head. "Acchh! We should never have hired him."

"Where's Mr. Barazza going?" she asked Giorgio as Barazza walked away from them.

"Making partiti, the deals. We need to make the deals with our allies, *Pantera*, the Panther and *Tartuca*, the Tortoise. They will help us to win."

"But we don't need any help. Storm is fast; he can win! Isn't this about being the fastest?"

"Is not only the speed we need, eh? There are many tricks our enemies will use to try and make us lose. We need to be prepared. You will see."

"Like what?"

"We will talk when Cesare finishes the deals. Come home; Maria will have lunch for us."

Angela did not feel like eating at all.

Chapter Nineteen

"You won't know your position until after you are on the track," Barazza told Angela as they sat at the table in the Leocorno stable. He was drawing a diagram on a scrap of paper. "The positions are decided by a mechanical device inside the judges' stand. As you know, if you get the tenth position, you start first, and those in the outside positions will try to crowd you out by sneaking close to the infield. You must beware of this. Watch out for the Owl's jockey, Valente. He is riding Stella."

"So that's his name. He's the one who spoke to me at the start of the Provaccia this morning."

"He spoke to you?" Barazza asked, raising one eyebrow.

"Well, he jeered at me. I couldn't understand what he was saying."

"Be careful of him. He is strong, and he will try to knock you off with his *nerbo*. The nerbo is the special whip of the Palio—made from ox hide. It is immortalized in our contrada's motto: *Faithful and strong is the weapon I hold in front of me.* You will receive yours when the parade is finished; they are handed out just before the beginning of the race." He took a drink of coffee. "Your metal helmet will protect you from the whips."

"Protect me?" Angela asked.

"Yes. The other jockeys will try to force you off your horse by hitting you with them."

Angela cringed at the thought. *This is not just a horse race! This is a win-at-all-costs out-and-out war!*

Libby entered the room with his great-grandson, Joey, in tow.

"Joey, it is time to dress," Giorgio said, glancing at his watch. Joey followed Giorgio into a back room.

"It is great honour for my Joey to be chosen as *comparsa*," Libby said, beaming. "Very great honour." He watched the boy leave, then crossed the room and joined Barazza and Angela at the table.

"Comparsa?" Angela gave Barazza a puzzled look.

"The comparsa is a group of young men chosen to represent the contrade in the parade," Barazza said. "Afterwards the young men pay homage to the Palazzo del

Governo and other important institutions of Siena in the Piazza del Duomo. It is indeed a great honour."

Joey emerged fifteen minutes later in a flourish of colour and finery that reminded Angela of her Renaissance studies. On his head perched an embroidered silk hat, and his shoulders were draped with a rich orange and white brocade cape. A pair of thick, orange velvet tights clung to his legs.

"You look *magnifico!*" Giorgio said, following him into the room. "As fine a young man as ever paraded for Leocorno."

Libby gave Joey a warm hug.

"It is after three," Barazza said, looking at his watch. "Time for the blessing of the horses."

"Ah, yes," Giorgio answered. "This is a very important ceremony."

"Storm is ready," Libby said, leading the horse out of his stall.

Angela gasped at the sight of Storm, who stood proudly, his richly embroidered bridle topped with a silk and feather plume bearing the unicorn symbol at its base. An elegant blood-red saddlecloth trimmed with gold was draped over his back, displaying a naked angel with blue and gold wings and a white scarf floating across one shoulder. His hooves were encircled with tiny bells. He whinnied softly when Angela approached and adjusted his blinder.

"Storm!" she said. "You look so beautiful!" She planted a gentle kiss on the end of his nose. He pranced lightly on his feet, the bells making soft tinkling noises.

"Where are we going?" Angela asked.

"Into our church, the San Giovanni Battista della Staffa," Giorgio answered.

"Right into the church?" Angela asked. "Storm's going into the church?"

"Yes. He is an honourable member of this contrada now."

"But what if he…you know…dumps in the church?"

"This is good! We believe this is good luck!"

Angela shook her head. *Only in Italy!*

The procession headed to the contrada church, followed closely by the devoted crowds. Storm was hesitant to go up the church steps and had to be coaxed by Libby and Angela.

The priest muttered a lot of Latin prayers followed by an emphatic phrase that was so loud it made Storm skittish.

"What was that last prayer?" Angela asked Libby, who had tears in his eyes.

"He say, 'Go, and return a winner!'"

"Is it over?" Angela whispered.

"Yes," Libby said. "We go now." He and Angela led Storm down the aisle, but suddenly the horse stopped.

"Storm, come on!" Angela whispered, pulling on his bridle. "Don't act up now." She tugged again, but Storm wouldn't move.

"Wait," said Libby, turning to look at Storm's rear end. "Ahhh!" He grinned, and Angela heard a great plop, plop. "Ahhh!" Libby turned and faced the altar, crossing himself. "Thank you! Thank you! Is our good luck!"

There was an outburst of cheering from the crowd seated in the church, followed by cheering from the group of onlookers outside when they realized what had happened. They grabbed partners and danced around in circles, patting their neighbours on the back. Storm continued down the aisle and out into the sunshine.

Giorgio led a large bay mare forward and motioned to Angela. "You will ride on this horse now, and our stableboy will lead you. It is the tradition. Storm must walk in the parade without his rider, to preserve his energy," he said.

Angela climbed onto the big bay, which was draped in medieval finery. A richly coloured embroidered blanket covered the mare's back from her shoulders to her rump. An ornate bridle and chest piece adorned the front of her body. Angela adjusted her silks, feeling like a character in a time-travel novel, and joined the procession as it made its way toward the Gothic-Romanesque cathedral at the crest of the hill. The grandiose parade of trumpeters, drummers and Renaissance-costumed riders moved toward the Piazza, stopping four times to display the elaborate skills of the flag throwers.

The mood of the parade was sombre, in great contrast to the cheering and revelry of the previous days. The sound of the trumpets and the notes of the Palio anthem rang in Angela's ears. She was sweating under the strong afternoon sun, her silks sticking to her damp skin. She swivelled on her mount to take in the rest of the parade. She looked around for Tony but couldn't find him.

Near the back rode seven horsemen, and behind them were six armoured riders with closed visors, whose horses were masked. The group of six represented the "dead" contrade that no longer existed. And the group of seven represented the seven contrade who weren't competing in this race but would run in the second race in August.

The parade lasted almost two hours. It was followed by a great waving of flags when an ox-drawn chariot carrying trumpeters, bell-ringers and four elderly men, who represented the historical ruling council, rode into the Piazza. They brought the beautifully designed Palio, the silk banner that would be proudly carried away by the winning contrada, and deposited it in the judges' stand.

Angela gazed at the banner as it billowed in the slight breeze that blew across the Piazza. A new banner was specially designed each year, and Angela thought this one even more beautiful than the ones from years past she had seen displayed in the different contrada buildings. She pictured her and Storm riding out of the Piazza del Campo with the banner unfurling behind them, followed by masses of cheering Unicorn members.

The butterflies in her stomach refused to subside. In fact, they were getting worse as the race neared. It was such a long-drawn-out affair—all this pomp and pageantry—why couldn't they just have the race?

Angela dismounted from the bay and followed Libby, Barazza and Storm into the municipal building where they would wait for the signal to emerge and begin the race. She began chewing her nails, something she hadn't done for years.

"Now remember, Angela," Barazza said, trying to reassure her, "be careful of the other riders, especially Valente. Don't let anyone push you to the outside. If you draw an outside spot, shoot for the inside. Do what you have to to get in there. Use your nerbo if you have to." He wiped the sweat from his brow. "Oh, and one more thing—whatever you do, don't come in second. It will bring dishonour to our contrada."

Angela stared at him incredulously. "Dishonour?"

Barazza nodded.

"Because I'm a girl?"

"No, no. Everyone is excited that you are our jockey. It's shameful for anyone to come in second."

"Why?"

"Because...it means you had a good horse to make it that far. So people think the reason you didn't come first must be because you didn't do your very best."

"But that's stupid. That's really stupid!"

Barazza shrugged. "It's a matter of pride."

Angela sighed and excused herself. She had to find the ladies' room.

She splashed cold water on her face and stared at herself in the mirror. *What have I got myself into?* She shook her head, took a deep breath, walked out and ran smack into a jockey coming out from the men's room next door.

"*Scusi,*" Angela said, quickly turning away. She glanced up and saw Valente looking down at her. *Of all the luck!*

He said something in Italian, a look of shock on his face. Angela didn't answer but started to walk away. He grabbed her arm, looked her up and down, and Angela felt her face heat up. She could hear the bell from the Mangia Tower calling the jockeys to the starting line.

Valente began yelling.

"I...I...only speak English," she said.

"English?" he scoffed. "English?"

Angela nodded.

"You are a girl!" He spat in disgust, still holding on to her arm. "You never make it through this race!"

"Yes, I will, damn it, and I'll win!" she shouted. "Now let go of my arm!"

Valente dropped her arm and spat on the floor. Angela glared at him and began to walk away. Valente called to some other jockeys in Italian. There was much shouting and arm waving, and everyone crowded around her speaking rapidly. She felt dizzy, then heard a loud voice shouting above the din.

Barazza pushed his way into the crowd, leaned forward and yelled something into Valente's face. Barazza grabbed Angela's arm and pulled her away.

"Are you all right?" he asked, putting his arm around her.

"I'm okay," she replied, straightening her tunic and smoothing her hair. "What did you tell him?"

"I told him I would cut off his ears and fry them for his mother's breakfast. Now come, Catarina has something for you."

Back in the main hall, Angela saw Catarina wheeling toward them. She wore a blue floral dress that looked as bright as her face. "I brought you this," Catarina said, reaching into her pocket. She produced a small brown velvet box and handed it to Angela. "Open it."

"This is for me?" Angela tentatively took the box and opened it. Inside was a silver butterfly brooch embedded with tiny seed pearls. Angela gasped. "It's beautiful, but it's way too expensive! I can't accept it." She handed it back to Catarina, who shook her head.

"No, it's for you. *Porta fortuna*, for luck. It was my mother's. She would want you to have it. I want you to have it, and my father wants you to have it."

"But I can't, Catarina. I wouldn't feel right."

"You're like a member of our family now," Barazza said.

Angela sighed and gave them both a hug. "Thank you, thank you. I'll treasure it." She pinned it onto her tunic.

"Good luck," Catarina said, giving her a thumbs-up.

"*Coraggio!*" Barazza said.

"I'll bring the Palio banner home to Leocorno!" Angela said.

Barazza smiled and wheeled Catarina out. "Come, we must hurry now."

Outside, the drum rolls began, signalling the jockeys to enter the track.

Chapter Twenty

A page appeared and summoned all the jockeys to the starting area. Nervously, Angela joined the others, who stood in line to be searched by the police. After that, each jockey was handed a nerbo. Angela grasped hers firmly with one hand and pushed down on her metal helmet with the other. As she clutched the leather whip, she repeated the words of the contrada's ancient motto: *Faithful and strong is the weapon I hold in front of me.*

She gasped as an attendant splashed her pants with cold water, a trick designed to give the jockeys a better grip on the horses. She mounted Storm. He danced back and forth and tossed his head.

At five minutes to seven, a gunshot sounded, signalling everyone to clear the track. Moments later, a second shot rang out, and the jockeys rode their horses onto the course.

Angela was overwhelmed by the sight of the huge crowd straining against the barricades, punching the air with their fists, swirling their flags and shouting.

Turning their mounts toward the Palazzo Publico, the jockeys raised their whips in salute and began their slow approach to the starting rope. A voice rattled off the starting position numbers.

"Giraffe: one, Wave: two, She-Wolf: three, Goose: four, Tortoise: five, Unicorn: six, Owl: seven, Shell: eight, Tower: nine, and Eagle: ten. Riders—take your positions!"

Tony has the inside track!

Angela was beside Valente in the middle of the pack. Confusion reigned as nervous horses jostled and shoved into position. Some jockeys had trouble controlling their jittery mounts. Angela kept a tight rein on Storm and sidled him into position six just as Valente reined in beside her. He raised his nerbo in a threatening gesture, and she glared back at him. Her mouth felt dry. She licked her lips. She adjusted her helmet. It felt too big, and its weight pressed down on her ears. Storm snorted and bounced his head up and down.

Tortoise's jockey nodded and saluted her with his whip. One of his front teeth was missing and his straight hair poked out from under his helmet. His mount was calm compared to the others.

Angela looked up into the evening sky. The sun cast long shadows across the red-tiled rooftops of the buildings surrounding the Piazza. The intense heat of the day still hung in the air.

Suddenly, Angela heard the thunder of approaching hooves and saw Eagle's horse gallop up to the front line. Then the rope dropped and they were off. Owl's horse shot to the inside, and Storm followed closely behind. Ahead of her, Valente began flailing at Eagle, his nerbo glancing off the shorter jockey's helmet. Tortoise and Goose pulled up on her right. Angela leaned low over Storm's neck.

"Go, Storm, go!" she shouted in his ear.

The San Martino curve loomed ominously ahead. As she drew up beside Valente's flank, he glanced back and lashed out with his nerbo. Instinctively, Angela ducked. Then pandemonium broke out.

Goose slammed sideways into the mattresses at the San Martino curve, unseating his rider. The force of the impact sent one of the mattresses sliding onto the track. Valente checked his mount to the left just in time.

Angela glanced quickly to her right, but She-Wolf was within inches of her flank. There was only one chance. Angela grasped Storm tightly with her knees, leaned over his neck and gave him his head.

"Jump!" she shouted, and Storm flew into the air, clearing the mattress easily. As he landed lightly on the other side, the crowd broke into a loud frenzy.

They slid into the next curve, struggling to hold the inside. Valente had pulled farther ahead, and She-Wolf was gaining on their right. Angela gave Storm his head down the stretch. Spectators leaned dangerously over the barricades, wildly waving flags inches from her head.

First lap done!

They passed the judges' box and thundered down toward the San Martino curve for the second time. Shell and Owl were neck and neck with Tortoise and Eagle, just ahead. Giraffe had fallen behind, so Tortoise and Eagle had the inside. Then Tortoise's jockey pushed Eagle into the wall, striking the jockey with the nerbo, forcing Eagle to fall back and give up his prime position.

As they neared the curve, Valente slid sideways and his horse stumbled. Angela took advantage and pushed Storm alongside. But Valente struck her with the nerbo as she passed, his glancing blow ringing off her metal helmet.

"Faster, Storm. Faster!" she shouted over the din of the crowd as she dug her heels into his sides. His ears swivelled back, and he lunged ahead with a burst of speed. Once again, they made it around the San Martino curve unharmed and raced toward the Casato corner. They galloped around it just behind Tortoise, who was in the lead, and Shell, who was running a close second. They roared past the judges' box where the Palio banner waved and headed toward the San Martino curve for the third time.

We are in third place with one lap to go!

Tortoise's horse had the inside advantage on the steep downward slope. But just then, Angela heard a loud snap, and Tortoise's mount sprawled onto the track. Shell collided catastrophically with them, littering the curve as Angela approached. There was no way around the mess of twisted jockeys and horses, and Angela braced herself for the crash. But Storm leaped into the air, barely clearing the sprawling heap.

The crowd roared as his hooves found clear ground on the other side. Owl skirted the wreckage and pulled up just behind them on Angela's right. As they raced into the Casato corner again, Valente began viciously whipping his horse in a fervent effort to catch them. He caught them as they rounded the corner and pushed Storm against an inside barricade. Angela's leg slammed into it, and her ankle twisted backward. She bent her other leg back over Storm's rump to avoid being crushed by Valente's horse. She lashed out with her nerbo and struck Valente squarely on his face. Blood spurted from a gash above his eye.

Storm bounced off the barricade, pulling free, and Angela gritted her teeth as pain flooded through her ankle. The crowd roared when Valente's horse pulled into the lead, but suddenly Tony's horse drew up on the inside, nostrils flaring, reaching for the finish line that loomed ahead.

"Go, Storm!" Angela screamed. "We're almost there!"

The three horses thundered down the track neck and neck. But when Tony pulled ahead, Valente reined in his horse. Barazza's words flashed through Angela's mind: *"It is shameful to come in second."* She tightened her knees and gave Storm his head. All she cared about at that moment was winning.

"We can do it, Storm! We can do it!"

With a sudden burst of speed, Storm crossed the finish line inches ahead of Tony. "We did it! We won the Palio!"

It had been less than ninety seconds since they had surged onto the course, but to Angela it had seemed like a lifetime.

The noise from the crowd was deafening. Flowers, hats and flags flew through the air. Spectators burst past the barricades and crowded in behind Storm. Angela felt him trembling. Suddenly, Libby appeared, pushing his way through the crowd, smiling broadly. He reached out, grabbed Storm's reins and led them toward the judges' box. The brightly coloured Palio banner unfurled in the wind.

Giorgio and Barazza were at her side. *"Magnifico!"* Giorgio shouted, jumping and laughing.

"*Brava, brava!*" Barazza yelled.

Angela grasped the banner and held it high above her head with both arms. Someone placed a garland of flowers around Storm's neck. Dozens of men and women reached up to touch his head and pull at his thick mane. They tugged at his bridle and stroked his neck. He buried his nose in Libby's shirtsleeve.

Angela winced at the pain in her ankle as contrada members pushed in against her. In the adrenalin rush of the race, she had forgotten about her injury. Now the pain flooded back.

Angela saw Tony's mount being led away but did not see him anywhere. She heard the Unicorn's contrada song in the distance. As she slid off Storm's back, Giorgio grabbed her hand. "Come on, you're going to be the centre of attention at the grand banquet! You need to get ready!"

It was a long evening full of celebration.

Chapter Twenty-One

Angela didn't sleep much that night. The partying and revelry on the streets continued until dawn, and the noise drifted up through her window, keeping her awake. Finally, she gave up trying to sleep and stumbled downstairs, rubbing her eyes and yawning. Aunt Maria was just getting up. She didn't have her apron on yet, and her hair fell down her back almost to her waist, its rich chestnut colour threaded with strands of silver. It reminded Angela of her mother, and Angela realized how much she missed her.

"Angie," Aunt Maria said, pulling a chair out from the table, "sit, I make you some breakfast. I'm really proud of you. All of Italy is proud." She pulled her apron down from the hook beside the stove and tied it around her waist. Picking some hairpins up from a dish on the counter, she pulled her hair back in a bun and began pinning it up. Angela watched her fondly.

"Aunt Maria," Angela said, "come and sit down. Forget about breakfast. Come and sit and talk."

Aunt Maria stopped, holding a hairpin in her mouth. "Huh? You want to talk? What is it, huh? Is Tony? You pregnant?"

Angela laughed. "No, Aunt Maria. I'm not pregnant. Come," she said, pulling out the chair beside her. "You're always looking after everyone. Sit for a while. Breakfast can wait."

Aunt Maria frowned and walked slowly over to the chair. "You okay, Angie?" she asked, leaning forward to look into Angela's face.

Angela lowered her eyes to the floor. "I should have listened to your advice about Tony."

"Aahh," Aunt Maria said, patting Angela's knee. "I see. Is okay, is okay. You make mistake, no make it again, huh?"

Impulsively, Angela jumped up from her chair and wrapped her arms around Aunt Maria. She was going to miss her.

That afternoon, Angela decided to give her mom a call. As she listened to the loud *brrriinng, brrriinng* at the other end of the line, she thought how much had changed since she had arrived in Italy.

"Hello?" She heard her mother's soft voice.

"Mom, it's Angie."

"Angie!" her mom exclaimed. "I'm so proud of you! Giorgio finally reached me, and I caught a rerun of the Palio on TV. You were amazing! Angie, the CBC called. They want to interview you when you get back. I'm so proud of you!"

"That's great!"

"Your dad would be so proud, Angie."

Tears stung Angela's eyes. She swallowed and said softly, "See you in a week. I miss you, Mom."

"I miss you too, Angie. Bye."

As soon as Angela hung up, the phone rang. It was Catarina. "Angie!" she said. There was excitement in her voice. "You have to come out. I have a surprise for you."

Catarina and Barazza were waiting outside in the yard when Giorgio and Angela pulled up.

"Guess what? Guess what?" Catarina exclaimed.

"What?" Angela asked.

"Come on!" Catarina said, spinning her wheelchair around and heading to the barn. Giorgio and Barazza went into the house, and Angela followed Catarina to the barn.

Catarina wheeled up the stable aisle, past Storm's stall. He was not yet back from the contrada stable. At the end of the aisle, she stopped, swung her wheelchair around and smiled at Angela. "Look!" she said, pointing to a stall. "Look in there!"

Angela walked up to the stall door and peered inside. A stocky brown mare with a long mane and a fluffy tail stood munching hay.

"This is Dina. Isn't she beautiful?" Catarina asked.

"Yeah! Is she yours?"

"All mine. Papa bought her for me to ride. What do you think?"

Angela opened the stall door and walked inside. She ran her hands over Dina's neck and withers and ruffled her forelock. "She's a sweetheart," Angela said. "Want to try her out?"

"Right now?"

"Sure, why not?"

"Well, I...I don't know."

"Does she have her own bridle?"

"Right there." Catarina pointed to a slender bridle draped over the seat of a tooled black saddle that sat atop the stall wall. "But...maybe we should get to know each other first."

"Riding is a good way," Angela said, slipping the bridle over Dina's head. Angela quickly saddled the horse, opened the stall door and led Dina out. "You better get changed," she said, glancing at Catarina's skirt.

"Okay, come in with me. I could use your help getting dressed. And I've got another surprise for you."

"Sure." Angela led Dina outside, looped the reins over the fence post and then followed Catarina inside to her room.

After Angela helped Catarina change clothes, Catarina wheeled over to her desk.

"Look," Catarina said, pulling a photo out from one of the drawers and handing it to Angela. "This is the other surprise."

The photo showed a man and woman standing beside two horses. The man, who looked like a young Mr. Barazza, had his arm around a woman that Angela recognized as her mother at a much younger age. She was smiling up at him.

"Papa and your mother must have had a thing going before she got married!"

"Your dad and my mom?" Angela couldn't believe it. "Where did you find this?"

"In an old photo album a couple of days ago."

"I wonder what happened between them."

Catarina shrugged. "They broke up, I guess. Your mom went to Canada. Papa has never mentioned it."

"Neither has Mom."

"Wouldn't it be neat if..." Catarina laughed.

"We could fix them up again?" They both laughed.

"What are you two laughing about?" Giorgio asked, walking in with Barazza.

"Nothing," Catarina said, putting the photo back in the drawer again. "Come outside and watch me ride my new horse."

Barazza smiled at her.

They went outside together, and Barazza lifted Catarina onto Dina as Angela unhitched the horse.

"Easy, girl," Catarina said. She walked Dina around the paddock, then gently urged her into a trot.

"*Brava, brava!*" everyone cheered. Catarina grinned.

Angela turned to Barazza and said, "There's still one thing I need to know about the Palio. Did I win it fair and square?"

"Of course you did."

"But Uncle Giorgio said you went to make partiti."

Barazza laughed. "With you riding, I didn't need to do that. No, I decide to go buy my Catarina this horse."

"What? You didn't make partiti*?*"

Barazza shook his head and smiled.

"Oh, I know." Angela nodded. "It's a matter of pride."

Ann Chandler lives in Vancouver, BC. She has an MFA in Creative Writing from UBC and has been published in magazines such as The Beaver *and* Reader's Digest. *This is her first published book.*